The Fastest Bov

Michael Hardcastle was
Yorkshire, and after leaving school he served in the
Royal Army Educational Corps in England, Kenya and
Mauritius. Later he worked for provincial daily news-
papers in a variety of writing roles, from reporter and
diarist to literary editor and chief feature writer. In
1988 he was awarded an MBE for his contribution to
children's writing.

His first children's book was published in 1966 and
since then he has written over a hundred more, but he
still finds time to visit schools and colleges all over
Britain to talk about books and writing. He now lives
near Hull.

by the same author

ONE KICK
KICKBACK
SECOND CHANCE
OWN GOAL
QUAKE
PLEASE COME HOME

GOAL KINGS
BOOK ONE: SHOOT-OUT
BOOK TWO: EYE FOR A GOAL
BOOK THREE: AND DAVEY MUST SCORE

The Fastest Bowler
in the World

Michael Hardcastle

faber and faber
LONDON · BOSTON

First published in 1996
by Faber and Faber Limited
3 Queen Square London WC1N 3AU
This paperback edition first published in 1997

Photoset by Avon Dataset Ltd, Warwickshire
Printed and bound in Great Britain by
Mackays of Chatham PLC, Chatham, Kent

A CIP record for this book
is available from the British Library

ISBN 0–571–17356–X

2 4 6 8 10 9 7 5 3

For Katherine, whose enthusiasm for cricket
happily knows no boundaries

One

'It's mine, all mine!' yelled Nick, leaping to his feet. 'Don't get in my way, Denis, whatever you do.'

Denis Demarco had no intention of moving by so much as a centimetre, let alone interfering with his best friend's ambition. He was perfectly content to remain sprawled on the boundary, watching others run all over the place and get hotter than ever.

Nick's gaze never wavered as he hurtled alongside the boundary rope. The fielder, he calculated, would never manage to catch up with the ball as it sped towards a point still some twenty metres to Nick's right. As it flicked over the line for yet another four Nick flung himself full-length and, with outstretched arm, succeeded in preventing it travelling any further. Then, as nonchalantly as possible, he got to his feet and lobbed the ball into the arriving fielder's hands.

'Thanks, son,' Kamran Aslam said, grinning. 'Wish I had your energy.'

'Wish *I* could bowl like you,' Nick told him fervently.

Kamran's eyebrows went up. 'Well, keep trying and you never know,' he remarked before effortlessly hurling the ball to his wicketkeeper.

'Hey, you did it, you actually talked to him – and he

actually talked to you!' Denis greeted him as Nick flopped back on to the grass beside him. His tone mixed mockery with admiration. 'So you can put a big red mark in your diary for today: "I spoke to my hero and he replied." Followed by several exclamation marks and maybe asterisks as well.'

'You're right! That's just what I'll do. Bet one day some cricket-crazy kid will write in his diary that *he* met Nick Freeland, legendary England fast bowler and holder of the world record number of wickets in Tests – 555 to be spot on. And he'll get my autograph as well.'

Denis just nodded. That was the sort of boast he'd heard innumerable times. But he never scoffed. He didn't really doubt that Nick would achieve some outstanding success in the game even if he failed to reach the highest of his ambitions. It had been hammered into Denis many times at home that 'real dedication to a genuine cause will always pay off in the end'. That hadn't exactly motivated Denis himself, as it was intended to, but he could believe it applied to others.

For the next few minutes they watched in silence as a tiring attack was put to the sword by exuberant batsmen intent on knocking up personal best scores before the declaration came.

'Why doesn't the skipper put your hero on again?' Denis said at last. 'He'd break this partnership. Even if he didn't, he'd keep the runs down.'

'Don't think he fancies his chances on this wicket,'

Nick told him without mentioning that he'd noticed Kamran shake his head distantly in apparent mute response to an appeal from his captain. 'I mean, there's nothing in it for him. And he can't improve his average in a friendly like this, can he?'

Denis gave him a shrewd look. 'But you'd want to bowl, wouldn't you, Nick? You'd just about break the skipper's arm getting the ball off him!'

'You bet! There'll never be a time when I don't want to bowl. I mean, if you're not whacking the ball down you can't take wickets, can you? Catches off other bowlers don't count with me.'

He switched his attention back to Kamran, unable to admit that he thought the Pakistan paceman was wrong to take a rest when he could go hurtling into action again, forcing the batsmen to duck and weave out of the way of his thunderbolts. Now that they were so well set they'd be bound to take a risk or two trying to hit him off his length. Even though it *was* a minor match, a benefit game for one of the players, he'd be facing these guys again later in the season in serious combat. So he might as well establish his domination over them now. A snick for a caught-behind was just as good as sending the middle stump cartwheeling out of the ground. Well, it was in these circumstances, anyway.

'I need an ice-cream – dying for one,' Denis announced. 'Want one?'

'Yeah, great idea. I'll come – '

'No, you keep watching the hero – don't miss one

precious moment. Never know what you might pick up, apart from the ball, I mean. You might even see him bowling again while I'm gone.' He lumbered to his feet. 'Anyway, I need some exercise. A walk to the van's better than nothing.'

Nick felt he was generous in refraining from commenting that any benefit Denis gained from that would instantly be cancelled out by consuming ice-cream calories. But, he reflected a few moments later, Denis must really have raced there and back, although he had been away long enough to reduce one cone almost to the brim.

Just as he reached out for his own refreshment Nick saw Kamran pounding towards him again in pursuit of the ball. Once more it beat him to the boundary. Nick deftly scooped it up and held it out to the bowler. 'Oh, and you can try my ice-cream as well, if you like,' he added, grinning.

Kamran nodded, flung the ball in a high parabola to his keeper and then took the proffered cone. To Nick's great surprise, the bowler bit so deep that most of the ice-cream seemed to disappear at one go. How could he swallow something so bitingly cold? Nick couldn't help wondering. But then, Asian people really liked hot food, didn't they, so maybe it worked for them with the opposite extreme, too.

'Thanks – needed that,' Kamran said, handing back the remains.

'You can, er, take it all, if you like,' said Nick, trying to keep any suggestion of irony out of his voice.

But there was a vigorous shake of the head in response. 'No way! Skipper would not approve at all. He'd bowl me into the grave for accepting bribes or something!'

'You shouldn't be fielding at third man, anyway,' Nick remarked impulsively. 'Any mis-timed drive like that is bound to get through. Just means a wasteful chase for you. Can't think why the skipper doesn't ask you to field in the slips.'

Kamran's dense eyebrows ascended. 'I can see you know your cricket, son. Pity you're not in our side today to tell the skipper how to run things. Oh – gotta go!'

His boundary conversation had been spotted by the captain who was gesticulating to his chief strike bowler to get back to his position and concentrate on the game. Ruefully, Nick turned his own attention to what was left of his ice-cream.

'Well, that should teach you not to be such a know-all in future,' Denis observed with a sly smile.

'Meaning?' Nick inquired, genuinely puzzled.

'Well, it was pretty obvious Kamran thought you were trying to show how smart you are, being a show-off. And he didn't like it. *Obvious*.'

Nick frowned. 'Not obvious to me, Den. *I* got the impression he recognized I know what I'm talking about and he agreed with everything I said. I mean, I wasn't trying to prove anything. I just said what I thought.'

'As you always do,' Denis remarked tonelessly.

'Doesn't always do you a lot of good, you know.'

Nick, who'd been lying full-length on his stomach, now raised himself on his elbows. 'Listen, Den, I don't know what you're getting at. I told you, I was just being myself. No point in being anything else, is there? It's the first time I've ever got to talk to the guy I regard as the best fast bowler in the world – which is what I'm going to be one day. So I've got to grab the chance to let him know I'm around, that I may still be a school boy, but I know as much about cricket as any professional. Well, *almost* any. You never know, I might need Kamran's help one day. He might even need mine! If he doesn't know I exist there'd be no chance of that, would there?'

Denis, still calmly licking his way into the cone, shrugged. 'Right, right, sorry I spoke. Don't get worked up about it, Nick. Just enjoy the match. That's what we're here for.'

At that moment, however, the players began to troop from the field. The opposition captain, leaning out of the pavilion window and clapping his hands to call his batsmen in, had declared.

'Right, that's it,' announced Nick, jumping to his feet and swallowing the final fragments of his cone. 'I'm not stopping to watch any more of this. Kamran will have his feet up in the pavilion for the next couple of hours. And *I* need some action. Got to think about my own match tomorrow. So let's go and get a bat and I'll work you over in the nets.'

'Oh, come on, you've had one bowling spell today,

let's give it a rest,' protested Denis. 'I'm enjoying this, doing absolutely damn-all on a beautiful day. Makes it even more beautiful, just watching other people work.'

'The entertainment value's zero now Kamran's stopped bowling for the day. I don't want to watch a bunch of no-hope trundlers just go through the motions because this is one of their mates' benefit match and nobody really cares who does what.' He paused as Denis plainly dithered about what to do next. 'Anyway, it'll cost you if you hang about any longer. Before long people will be out with buckets collecting spare cash from everyone for the beneficiary's benefit – hey, good phrase that, isn't it?'

Whatever it was, it provoked Denis into rising but he couldn't resist another grumble. 'Listen, you should be glad to chuck a few coins into a bucket. You'll be expecting *millions* to do it for you if – sorry, when! – you do all the things you say you'll do and become the world's top bowler. So – '

'*Fastest*, not just top,' Nick corrected him. 'Anyway, can't afford anything else today, not after buying these wrist-bands. Look great, don't they?'

'Well, everybody's bound to notice 'em. Orange-and-blue is a bit spectacular to say the least. But I don't know why you wasted your money on them. I mean, you don't sweat that much, do you, not normally. So what's the point?'

'The point, my dumb old mate, is that they'll give the batsmen the idea that I *am* working up a sweat, a

sweat caused by the speed and energy of my bowling,'
Nick grinned. 'And that'll scare 'em half to death!'

'Ah, but if you just looked cool and confident, but
still bowled like, like a guided missile, well, that would
be better still,' Denis pointed out.

But his advice went unheard. Nick Freeland had
broken into a sprint so that he could arrive at the
distant nets full of running.

Two

'Just do your best,' the Trimdon skipper advised as Nick clattered down the pavilion steps, already wind-milling his bat in his left hand.

'Do I ever do anything else?' Nick called back over his shoulder before deciding that a dignified silence would have been better. After all, there was no point in antagonizing Craig, whose opinions were the ones that mattered in team-selection meetings. Mr Highton, sports supremo as well as maths teacher, was forever pointing out that in the field his own power passed to the captain.

'If you can keep your end up I'll get some runs on the board, no danger,' Steven Lindley greeted him when he reached the wicket. 'Still seven overs to go, so anything is possible. Oh, and don't back up too far when I'm on strike. This lot'll have your bails off in a split-second without a word of warning.'

Nick had a lot of respect for Steven's ability once he'd got over his usual attack of jitters at the beginning of an innings. Now, with 36 runs to his credit out of Trimdon's lamentable total of 75 for 6, Steven should be ready to launch himself into a real assault on Rochbury's bowlers. Unless Trimdon's total reached at least 120, Nick calculated, they wouldn't have much chance of winning this inter-school match, however well he himself bowled. But what he didn't know, because Mr Highton wouldn't tell him yet, was whether he would even be called on to bowl.

Rochbury had brought back their opening bowler in an attempt to get rid of the obdurate Steven, but his first delivery was over-pitched and the batsman stepped out to drive it confidently to the mid-off boundary, a shot that plainly gave him a lot of satisfaction, judging by the expression on his thin features. Nick patted his own bat to indicate applause. He'd be quite happy for Steven to play every remaining ball if, as now seemed likely, he was hitting form. His confidence in his own batting wasn't nearly as high as it ought to be, he knew. People kept telling him he'd do a lot better for himself as a cricketer if he could turn his tens and teens into thirties and forties and thus have claims to be an all-rounder instead of simply a fast bowler who might pick up a few easy runs. The problem was, he argued, that he was never sent in to bat until it was too late for him to get a good score; and invariably he'd been given orders by coach or skipper to 'hit out or get out, no glory in just sticking around to waste time'. Another problem was that, basically, he didn't care enough about his batting: all he wanted to do was to get rid of opposition batsmen. 'Bowlers,' he heard it said often enough to recognize the truth of it, 'win matches.'

Steven had to turn to defence again for the next two balls, the second of which was a good attempt at a yorker that almost squeezed under his bat. He looked exasperated and Nick guessed that whatever was served up to him next he'd go for a run. Correct! Nick was racing towards the other end almost before the batsman was into his stride after flicking the ball away to leg. 'Two, make it two!' Steven yelled; and they made it.

The bowler was looking as displeased as Nick would in similar circumstances and he muttered something and gesticulated in Nick's direction. Nick grinned. He didn't know what all that was about but he always enjoyed upsetting rival bowlers whoever they were. He didn't even know the boy's name. Rochbury were new opponents for Trimdon and therefore an unknown quantity. All that Nick could be sure of was that none of their players had yet been selected for the county youth team. Because it was his ambition to get into that side, Nick made sure he knew who his rivals might be and which schools they represented.

The next ball was on a length and Steven dealt with it well, turning it past short square leg. There was surely a run in it but, after starting off, Steven suddenly hesitated and then, putting up a hand to say 'Stop!,' edged back into the protection of his crease.

Nick, already charging down the wicket, braked, stumbled, lost his balance, somehow recovered it and by a fraction of a second beat the fielder's throw and was safe.

While Nick glared angrily down the wicket at

Steven, who was shrugging an apology, the bowler asked the heavens: 'How *lucky* can you get?' He didn't appear to get an answer but plainly didn't doubt what it should have been.

Off the last ball of the over Steven collected an easy single and then made a point of saying to Nick: 'Sorry about that close escape. But I remembered in time that fielder's a left-hander, so he wouldn't have to turn to pick up and throw in.'

'Oh, right,' Nick conceded, properly impressed by that revelation. It would never have occurred to him to try to memorize such details about opponents, and especially opponents they were meeting for the first time. 'But we've got to grab every run we can, you know. We haven't got a big enough total to bowl at if we're going to win.'

Steven's expression switched to one of irritation. 'Listen, Freeland, I've been playing in this team for years. You've only just got in, you haven't done anything yet. So don't tell me what's going on.'

Nick turned away to take up the non-striker's position. He wanted to tell Steven that, just because he was a newcomer, it didn't make his opinion any less valid. Furthermore, Steven himself hadn't shown any sense of urgency in his earlier batting so probably it needed someone else to remind him of the importance of runs in the final overs.

As if still bothered by Nick's comment Steven swished and missed at the first two balls of the new over from Rochbury's other returned opening bowler, a tall, pacey, sandy-haired boy with a whippy, high-arm action. This was Vigor Allan, rather unrealistically known to all his friends as Red, who had already had a trial for the county. His dismay at not getting Steven's wicket with his first two deliveries soared to shrieked disbelief when his appeal for lbw was turned down next ball. Hands on hips, trunk stretched forward at 45 degrees, he remained rooted to the centre of the pitch, glaring at his opponent, until his captain came up to put an arm around his shoulders and gently turn him back towards his mark. Nick viewed the scene with the greatest possible interest, not least because he knew he'd have been just as confident of getting a decision in his favour with that ball. So perhaps Steven's luck was really in and now he could try a few lusty blows to improve Trimdon's score and perhaps get his own 50.

It seemed so. Off the fourth ball Steven got a thick outside edge with the ball eluding third man and hitting the boundary wall with a fearsome thwack; the fifth brought him a streaky two; and the batsmen ran a single for a leg-bye off the last ball. Red's facial colouring matched his nickname.

'You trying to keep the strike from me or what?' Nick grinned as the batsmen crossed. But his attempt at restoring a friendly relationship with his team-mate was unrewarded. Steven didn't even deign to look at him. Perhaps, Nick thought charitably, he didn't hear me.

What Nick heard next was the voice of the opening

bowler excitedly yelling: 'How's that, then?' And he hadn't even let go of the ball!

In his eagerness to persuade Steven to have a go at whatever kind of ball he received Nick had backed up too far and the bowler, seizing his chance of getting rid of one opponent, broke off his run and deftly flipped off the bails to claim a run-out. It was the sort of gamesmanship Nick couldn't believe would be carried out in a schools match at this level.

Furious, he turned to see the feared, ominous sight: the umpire's finger was raised.

'But, but he never warned me!' Nick protested. 'I mean, it should – '

'He didn't have to and – ' said the umpire in the same instant that the bowler shouted: 'Yes, I did, I told you the last over I bowled. You've been trying this on every ball I've bowled. Well, now you've got what you deserve. So, on your way, you're OUT!'

'Sorry,' murmured the umpire to Nick. 'But it's within the laws, so I have no alternative. You were well out of your ground, you see.'

Nick was too angry to say anything sensible but he knew not to argue or utter threats. That had been drummed into him at the earliest possible age by his mother. 'You can never, *never* win in those circumstances, so don't try. Just think, Nicholas, *think*. That's why you've got a brain. The time to put things right will come one day.' Well, he told himself as he stalked away, tonight he'd tell her he'd not forgotten her advice. It would be something to trade with next time he was out of favour at home.

'They won't get away with it,' Steven muttered belligerently as Nick passed him on the way back to the pavilion. 'Charlie will bounce them to hell and back. They won't know what's hit 'em.'

Charlie Yorke was Trimdon's top-rated bowler and lately had been developing a fairly successful line in short-pitched deliveries that batsmen had trouble in fending off, particularly if they weren't tall. Rather to Nick's surprise, Mr Highton seemed to be encouraging that line of attack. Nick, on the other hand, believed that every fast bowler should concentrate almost exclusively on line and length, forcing batsmen to play every ball and frustrating them when they couldn't score. That way the batter would be more likely to take risks, and so lose his wicket. But Mr Highton appeared uninterested in that argument. Which, Nick was convinced, was the reason why he himself wasn't being given a chance to open the bowling with Charlie or in his place.

'Did he warn you he was going to do that?' Mr Highton demanded to know as he waited for him in front of the pavilion.

'He said he did – previous over,' replied Nick with a shrug. 'But I didn't hear him.'

'Well, it's unbelievable,' the sports master went on. 'You wouldn't get anyone doing that in a Test match even if the Ashes depended on it! Kids with no idea of the laws wouldn't do it if there was money on it!'

Nick wasn't sure about that but he wasn't going to

say so. Sometimes Mr Highton had weird ideas about what should go on during a cricket match even though he mostly measured everything by Test standards.

'I'll be able to get my own back, though, won't I?' Nick suggested inspirationally. 'I mean, that's if I open the bowling, Mr Highton.'

'Oh no, we're not getting into the revenge business, Nick, definitely not!' was the sharp response. 'We're not descending to their level. We play cricket, true cricket, even if they don't care to.'

Nick swallowed hard, realizing he'd miscalculated badly. Not only had he been cheated out of his wicket, as he saw it, but now he might not be allowed to bowl at all. Old Highbrow Highton was quite capable of keeping him out of the attack altogether just to make certain he didn't attempt to gain what he'd regard as his revenge.

'Didn't manage any runs, did you, young man,' the teacher added, twisting the knife. 'We could have done with a few more on the board, you know. And – oh dear! Oh, my good night.'

He'd broken off because another wicket had fallen. Charlie Yorke had taken Nick's place but he was still there. It was Steven, Trimdon's remaining hope for a good total, who was out. Unsettled by Nick's dismissal, he rashly attempted to follow one flashing cover drive, which brought up his 50, with another, failed to get to the pitch of the ball and edged a catch to slip. Eight wickets were now down for only 90 and Rochbury's players, naturally enough, were jubilant.

They were convinced it was their day and so the match was as good as won.

'Well done, Steven,' Mr Highton congratulated his batsman effusively. 'That was an excellent half-century.'

'Should have been a lot more runs out there for us,' Steven muttered darkly, his glance taking in Nick who was still standing beside the sports master.

'Well, don't blame me,' Nick replied instinctively. 'I never faced even one ball, so I had no chance of scoring.'

'Exactly!' remarked Mr Highton, turning away to follow Steven into the pavilion and presumably continue their conversation there.

Just what had been meant by that comment Nick didn't know, except that it plainly wasn't sympathetic. Yet no player could have been unluckier than himself, Nick believed: run out without facing a ball in circumstances almost anyone else would describe as gamesmanship. So why was he being treated more as a culprit than a victim? He went in to take his pads off and get something to drink.

The heatwave was still in full blast and even such a short spell in the middle induced a thirst. It must, he thought, be tough to bowl out there. No wonder Rochbury were so eager to remove their opponents and have a rest with a long, cool drink. Steven and Mr Highton were still in a conspiratorial huddle at the back of the room and Nick wasn't going to risk disturbing them. So he picked up a can of fruit juice and sauntered outside again. Craig Gooding, the captain, was lazily watching play from a fallen tree that had been carved into a bench-type seat. Nick went to join him.

'So what d'you think, then?' Nick opened up conversationally.

'About what?' Craig replied, not switching his gaze from the action. 'Our total? Their bowlers? Steven's batting? Your dismissal? Johnny Highton's teaching methods? My plans for next season?'

'Whatever.' Nick had deliberately been vague when he asked his question but hadn't expected such an odd response. Because Craig was a couple of years ahead of him at school, and therefore he didn't know him very well, he had simply hoped to learn something about his captain's attitudes. But now he sensed Craig didn't really want to discuss anything with him. Which was doubly unfortunate because he'd been hoping to steer the conversation round to his own prospects of being invited to bowl early in the innings.

'I think they're a better side than Johnny Highton was told they were,' was the latest unhelpful reply.

'Yeah, but we don't know what their batting's like, do we?' Nick persisted. 'Could be that Charlie will knock 'em over like nine-pins inside a few overs – well, Charlie and Adam, anyway. Unless, er, you're putting yourself on first with Charlie.'

'Maybe.'

That laconic rejoinder was so dismissive that Nick knew there was no point at all in trying to continue with this line of talk. In raising the matter of whether Craig might bowl himself he'd simply been flying a kite; and it had been shot down with one word. He had learned nothing whatsoever of the skipper's plans. Always assuming, he told himself, that Craig Gooding *had* a plan. From the little he'd seen of Craig's medium-pace drifters Nick didn't have a high opinion of his bowling; but, like many another batsman who turned his arm over occasionally, Craig considered himself to be a genuine all-rounder.

'Oh, good blow, Charlie, good blow!' Craig sang out as his opening bowler leaned back and crashed the ball high over point's head, the sort of stroke any batsman would have enjoyed playing. Nick joined in the applause.

Trimdon's total crept up by singles after that for a couple of overs but just when it seemed that 120 was in reach the innings came to an abrupt end. Charlie was run out attempting a hopeless sprint with the ball in the fielder's hands; and next ball Adam's middle stump was uprooted by Red Allan's finest delivery of the match.

Nick wondered what Craig really thought about Trimdon's chances of winning now, but he wasn't going to risk another snub. All he could hope was that he himself would get a chance to do some damage to the Rochbury batting order.

'We've got a lot of work to do, a huge amount,' Mr Highton told his assembled team with the usual teacher's repetition (as if we never take anything in on the first telling, Nick often reflected). 'We've let ourselves down with our batting, so we've got to make amends with our bowling and fielding. Catches win matches, don't they? Never forget it.'

Nick had expected more in the way of exhortations to do their best for the school and their own reputations but the maths master left it at that. He didn't, Nick noted, wish them luck. But perhaps that wasn't his style. This was only Nick's second match under Mr Highton's managership, so he still had a lot to learn about the man. In the classroom he was normally fairly reserved, favouring only those who thoroughly understood his calculations and equations. Nick was still struggling to make progress in the business of mathematics.

Rochbury began with the confidence to be expected of a team facing a modest total and with a seemingly harmless wicket to bat on. Charlie Yorke's opening over put the batsmen under no pressure whatsoever and they scored off every ball, except one which might easily have been adjudged a wide. Nick, fielding at long leg, where he could expect plenty of work at this rate, wondered what instructions Charlie had received from the boss, if any. Mr Highton could hardly have told him simply to do his best: Charlie was renowned for his enthusiasm in all circumstances. For that reason alone, it was going to be difficult for Nick to take his place as first-choice strike bowler for the school.

The score mounted rapidly, with no hint of a chance from either batsman, and Nick for one was beginning to sweat freely with all the chasing he was doing to prevent further boundaries. Surely, he argued silently, Craig must make a change. What's more, the skipper had to be aware of Nick as one of his options, for his fielding was rewarded from time to time with congratulatory claps from Craig at first slip. Moreover, although he was two years younger than nearly every other player, he'd been included in the team by the selectors (really Mr Highton, another master and Craig) as 'a fast bowler of real promise' according to the cricket report in last term's school magazine.

But Charlie and Adam continued to toil away. Then Charlie flung himself to his right in a great effort to grab what would have been a brilliant catch off his own bowling, but the ball eluded him as he fell awkwardly. When he got to his feet, his agony was plain even to someone fielding several metres away. It was his bowling hand that had suffered, and when Nick arrived to see the extent of the damage even the umpire was looking sickened.

'No, no, son, *don't* try to bend it back. That'll need re-setting if I'm any judge,' he murmured. 'Come on, let's get you off to hospital and the X-ray department.'

'Must have broken it to be sticking out at that angle,' Steven remarked morbidly; and no one disagreed.

It must mean, Nick told himself, that I'll get to bowl next. But it didn't. Craig casually tossed the ball to Tristram Morton to complete the over with instructions to 'keep it tight'. Nick swallowed his disappointment. There was nothing to be gained, he knew, from asking the skipper why he hadn't been invited to bowl. For one thing, Craig would have the perfect answer that he was about to find out if the wicket would take spin. So far, only pace had been tried in this match.

Tris's off-spin, however, was no more effective than speed in curbing the runs and Rochbury's opening pair continued to prosper. It was beginning to look as though they'd win the match on their own, inflicting on Trimdon the humiliation of a ten-wicket defeat. All he could console himself with was the thought that, as he'd neither faced a ball nor bowled one, he couldn't in any way be blamed for such failure.

Then, as the field changed at the end of an over with Rochbury more than half-way to their target of 112, Craig crooked an imperious finger in Nick's direction. 'If Adam doesn't make a breakthrough in this over I'll give you a go in his place,' the captain said. 'He needs a rest, I expect.'

It was hardly the most uplifting way of being told he was getting his chance at last, but Nick was in no position to complain. Not for the first time in his short playing career he was in the unfortunate position of wanting a team-mate to fail before he himself could succeed. As it happened, he almost succeeded in helping Adam to collect his first wicket. Rochbury's more forceful opening batsman flashed fiercely at a wide delivery and got a top edge. The ball went up in a high curve. Nick, patrolling the boundary at third man, sprinted forward. Because it went so high the ball began to drop steeply and Nick knew he wasn't going to reach it. All the same, he dived full-length in an effort to get a hand under it. It wasn't really a missed chance but his dive made it look like one.

Nick gave a rueful shrug and spread his hands wide to Adam after throwing the ball back. Adam, far more easy-going than Charlie, responded with a thumbs-up to show that he appreciated Nick's efforts. It proved to be his last chance of getting a wicket and remaining part of the attack.

'Do your best, we need it,' Craig remarked when he threw the ball to Nick at the end of another fruitless over by Tris, who appeared to be getting no turn at all. It seemed to be the captain's only phrase, Nick reflected, as he paced out his run with his usual heavy stride. Lately he hadn't been getting it quite right and several times he'd had to wheel away at the point of delivery, much to the chagrin of his captain in the Arkenley Cricket Club's second XI. The last thing he wanted today was to let Craig and Mr Highton suspect he wasn't capable of measuring out his own run-up.

The batsman, he saw, was constantly fiddling with the peak of his fairly stylish claret-and-blue cap, which perhaps he imagined might suggest to the half-knowledgeable that he was under consideration for a West Indies youth side. He was the one with a tendency to flash at anything wide of the off-stump. However, there wasn't much point in Nick trying to tempt him into that shot: Craig was allowing him only a single slip – himself. As usual, Nick's aim was to

23

shatter the stumps. No batsman could appeal against that dismissal.

No other fielder was close enough for Nick to practise his bowling action in the way that all the professionals did before sending down the first ball. He licked his dry lips and fleetingly wondered why he felt nervous; it wasn't like him. In so many things he'd been told often, 'Well, you don't lack confidence, do you?' It was true. But for some reason it wasn't present at the moment and he didn't know the reason.

Everything about his approach was right: twenty-two strides, slight curve from the left, arriving as close to the stumps as physically possible, arm well back, shoulder pointing straight down the pitch. But then – the ball just went! How it came to leave his hand like that Nick would never know.

And the batsman, seeing it coming straight for his head like an all-destroying missile, ducked under it. Which was just as well for otherwise it might have removed his brains as well as the colourful cap. And the ball hadn't bounced, hadn't touched the ground in any way.

'A beamer!' the umpire cried. 'What d'you think you're playing at, bowler?!'

'I'm sorry, sorry, sorry!' Nick exclaimed. 'I don't know what happened. I – '

He tried to signal an apology to the batsman, who had advanced down the pitch and was looking at him with venom. But he knew that it was the umpire and his own skipper who had to be placated. If the umpire believed that it had been Nick's intention to bowl like that then he'd insist on Trimdon's captain taking him off immediately.

'Let's have a look at your hand – yes, your right hand,' the umpire ordered to Nick's astonishment. Then, when it was displayed to him palm up, he went on: 'Do you normally sweat a lot?'

'Er, no, not normally, but maybe it's just nerves today,' Nick responded, grasping the chance he'd been offered to excuse his conduct. 'It's only my second match for the first XI, you see.'

'Well, if you throw the ball at a batsman like that again it'll be your last match for the school, believe me,' the umpire told him. 'I'll overlook it this time, but never again. Understand?'

'Yes, sir.' Nick had never in his life called an umpire 'sir' and, like the beamer, didn't know why he did it. Still, it had the required mollifying effect on the tall, stooping retired teacher.

'Very well. Go and start the over again. And remember, I wouldn't allow even an *Australian* opening bowler to get away with sending down a beamer.'

Because of the halt in play, and the length of conversation between umpire and bowler, Craig Gooding strolled across to inquire what was going on.

'Just a slip up, Craig. Sorry about it,' Nick responded. 'I'll get it right with the next ball.'

'You'd better,' the skipper murmured, employing another of his stock phrases.

Nick dried his palms again on the seat of his trousers and ostentatiously rubbed the ball against his thigh. It hadn't been new at the start of the match and so had little enough shine now, but the action helped the bowler feel better if nothing else. Suddenly, the next ball had become the most important in his entire life. It wouldn't matter at all whether it troubled the batsman or even took his wicket. All that mattered was that he delivered it properly and got it to hit the pitch in the right place. Another mistake like the last one and he might never play real cricket again as long as he lived. All of that went through his mind as he turned, paused fractionally and then began his measured run to the wicket.

The ball pitched perfectly, just where he wanted it to, and then moved away off the seam as the batsman, unsettled by his first experience of Nick's bowling, prodded forward tentatively. He got, as Nick had hoped, an edge, a thin edge, and the ball flew at waist height to where second slip would have been. But, of course, that area was vacant and so the ball continued unhindered to be met by the inrushing third man. Nick, as he always did, flung his arms high in the air and then down again in the manner of someone about to make a salaam or prayer. If only he'd been given a second slip . . .

'Glad to see you know how to bowl properly,' said the umpire under his breath when Nick walked past him. It was the most unexpected comment he'd ever received. Normally no umpire would dream of commenting on a player's performance in this way. If nothing else, it suggested a degree of bias which an umpire would not wish to possess, let alone display. But the words were uttered so softly that Nick was sure no one else could possibly have heard. He didn't feel it was appropriate to reply but he did glance at the man and give him a brief nod.

Craig, too, was expressing his approval by clapping silently with his hands above his head. Perhaps, Nick decided, the skipper also recognized that he'd erred in not giving his fast bowler a slip cordon. If someone else got a snick like that and thus another catching chance was missed then he'd have to point out his needs to his captain.

Because the lucky batsman had taken a single off that away-swinger Nick now had to adjust his line for the left-hander. In the past he'd tried a few times to bowl round the wicket to any left-hander he encountered but it hadn't worked well for him. It felt uncomfortable. Thinking about it later, he wondered whether part of the problem was that he couldn't get as close to the stumps as he normally did bowling over the wicket. Now and again he promised himself he'd discuss the matter with a really experienced pace bowler. Kamran, of course, would be the perfect choice.

Once again he found just the right length but this time the batsman was quick enough to drop his hands softly to stun the ball. He might have turned it to leg off his hips for there was no movement off the pitch with this delivery. Nick, however, was well pleased. He was sure now he'd found his customary rhythm. Soon, he'd work up to his full pace. That's when he'd need more attacking field placings, always supposing Craig was prepared to provide them.

With the final ball of his first over Nick got the wicket his team so desperately needed. Rochbury's captain, the right-hander, was facing him again when Nick produced the best weapon in his entire armoury, a yorker that fizzed under the raised, aimless bat and smashed down the off-stump. Nick leapt high with glee – and the rest of the team went up with him. None of the Trimdon players believed they were going to win this match (after all, Rochbury needed only a further 28 runs) but at long last they had something to celebrate.

'Great ball!' Craig came to tell him, slapping him heartily on the back. It was, Nick believed, the best he'd ever bowled, but instinct warned him not to say so. It was vital for his future in the school team that the skipper should feel he could rely on Nick Freeland now to bowl an unplayable ball at regular intervals! The last thing in the world he wanted was anyone to suppose it was a fluke.

He retreated to the mid-wicket boundary, mulling over what was undoubtedly the most dramatic over of his life from beamer to yorker. In fact, he should have had two wickets to his name instead of just one for two runs. Still, he'd done something no other Trimdon bowler had managed. Tris Morton, for one, certainly wasn't going to emulate him. Twice in the next six deliveries Nick was powerless to prevent the ball rocketing past him and over the boundary as Rochbury's left-hander swung fiercely against woeful bowling. At this rate, Nick reflected, Rochbury would get the necessary runs before he himself got a chance to bowl again!

'Come on, get another, get another!' Nick ordered himself as he caught the ball slung to him by Steven and walked back to his mark. He was going to continue bowling over the wicket to the left-hander, but wished he'd practised another method. His aim, however, was good enough to force the batsman to defend until the final ball of the over. This time, with the ball suddenly swerving away from him, he tried to cut, edged it – and somehow retained his composure as the wicketkeeper fumbled the ball and dropped it.

'Oh, no!' Nick lamented. Even though the in-swinger was unplanned, all that counted was the missed chance. His analysis could have read 2 overs, 1 maiden, 2 runs, 3 wickets; instead the final figure was still the one. It didn't occur to him he'd bowled the first maiden of the innings.

'Sorry!' the keeper signalled and Nick just shrugged. But at least he'd worried the batsman again into making a rash stroke. His line and length were all they should be. His rhythm was fine.

The skipper, he saw, seemed to be having a problem. Adam, whom he was talking to, was shaking his head, plainly unhappy about bowling again. Tris was being taken off so, with no one else he could trust to take over, Craig decided to bowl himself. It appeared to Nick he hadn't much faith in what he was trying to do, for his fielding arrangements were distinctly casual.

Rochbury sensed they were on to a good thing. They were right. Craig failed to find a length with his medium-pace cutters which barely deviated from a straight line and the batsmen helped themselves to easy pickings. Rather to Nick's chagrin, the winning run was scored off him in the next over, a streaky single that the keeper ought to have prevented.

Nick, walking off the field with Steven, wondered what Mr Highton would have to say about their performance. He was hardly the type to murmur some sympathy and wish them better luck next time. If he were to single anyone out for praise – apart from Steven – then it ought to be himself. After all, he hadn't let them down with the bat and he *had* taken the only wicket to fall. He'd bowled well. Surely none of that could be ignored.

But it was. Nick was the first player the maths master spoke to even before they could get into the dressing-room. 'Thought I told you not to retaliate,' he began cuttingly. 'So what did you think you were doing with that beamer?'

Nick felt the colour draining from his face. 'But it was an accident! A mistake! Just slipped out of my hand and – '

'Not what the umpire thought, so far as I could see.

Obviously he gave you a warning. Quite right! We're not having that sort of conduct in my team, I can tell you.'

Nick could sense his entire world collapsing about him. The bleakness in Johnny Highton's expression extinguished his hope that his slip would be overlooked. Forgiveness wasn't in the manager's make-up.

'Well, I'm sorry, really sorry, Mr Highton,' Nick tried to assure him. 'I did apologize to the batsman – oh, and the umpire. It won't happen again, I promise.'

'That's true. It certainly won't happen again, young man,' was the master's parting shot as he turned away to enter the pavilion.

Three

'Ah, so you've seen sense at last, have you, and changed your game?' Nick's father greeted him as he came into the kitchen. 'I always suspected it wouldn't really last, this obsession with cricket. No money in it and – '

'What're you going on about?' Nick cut in, genuinely puzzled. For once his father's attempts at witticisms made no sense at all.

'Well, unless I'm very wide of the mark, you don't play cricket in shorts, not even on a glorious summer's day. So I deduce you must be up to something else. Sunbathing perhaps, or some other idle pursuit?'

Nick switched the kettle on to make some coffee and slipped slices of bread into the toaster. He'd hoped to have breakfast on his own so that he could pay total attention to the county cricket scoreboard in the *Telegraph*. But he couldn't ignore his dad who, after all, funded his unceasing cricket expenses. All the same, it was irritating to have to defend his chosen sport. It was a pity his mother wasn't present. Jeff Freeland had long ago realized he was on a losing wicket when it came to discussing cricket with his wife, who was an all-rounder in the national women's team. But Nick also knew he was lucky to have parents who, so far as he could tell, disagreed completely on only one subject.

'If you must know, I'm playing tennis with Denis – and OK, no jokes please just because it rhymes! He's as fanatical about tennis as I am about bowling so he lets me bowl at him because I bash tennis balls back at him across the net.' He paused in buttering the toast and then added: 'Actually, I really like the game – but I haven't let Denis work that out yet.'

'Well, it's good to see you take a broader view of life at last,' his father said, sliding some complicated looking papers into his briefcase. 'Right, I must go and earn the cash to pay for all your pleasures, Nicholas. Want a lift to wherever you're going? I suppose I could make a minor diversion.'

Nick shook his head. 'No thanks. Denis's dad is picking me up. He's got a day off himself and is off to an auction or something at a nearby hotel.'

In fact, the pick-up was sooner than expected. Nick was still on the second slice of toast when Denis came charging in to ask him why he was still lazing around the breakfast table when he himself had been up for hours, preparing mentally for the great match due to take place on the Arkenley Sports Club courts within the next half-hour.

'No need for mockery,' Nick replied. 'Any future world-class bowler has to get himself into the right mental as well as physical mood before a Test match. That's all I said, and it's true. Not like your casual knock-around stuff at your game. If – '

'Yes, mate, but I play for pleasure, sheer pleasure,' Denis pointed out. 'I have no ambitions to display myself at Wimbledon or Flushing Meadow; wouldn't have even if I had the talent. So – '

The hoot of the car horn interrupted the argument, but only until they were seated in Mr Demarco's Alfa Romeo where the driver himself was perfectly content to listen to the badinage between his son and his friend without breaking in once. But then, he had no sporting interests of his own.

Denis's shape always suggested he couldn't be much of an athlete but the power of his serve had to be experienced to be believed. Nick was always thankful if Denis's first serve failed to cross the net, for only then did he feel he had a chance of winning the point. His own serve was still pretty moderate and he relied for success on his speed round the court and stamina in a long set. When the chance came he was also working on a top-spin return that might soon take an opponent by surprise.

'Let's knock up first, OK?' he said as soon as they arrived, knowing that Denis preferred to get into a game immediately, doubtless because his own stamina on a warm day was suspect.

'Just two minutes, then, that's all. With all your exercise at cricket you shouldn't need to warm up. You just want to delay the inevitable defeat, I know you.'

'Rubbish!' Nick took a yellow ball from his bag and served from where he was standing. It ricocheted from the low wall below the netting and Denis deftly caught it instead of hitting it back. 'I'm ready to start now if that's what you want. You've got to have every advantage you need, Den. Don't want you to have any complaints.'

Denis grinned. Things were always more competitive when Nick was being sarcastic. He himself felt in particularly good form, for he'd beaten another friend very easily in a club competition the previous weekend, though he wasn't going to mention that to his present opponent.

Rather generously, Nick conceded that Denis could serve first without the bother of tossing up for choice of ends or anything else. A few minutes later he was wishing he'd stuck to their usual arrangement because Denis couldn't have started better, winning his own two service games to love and breaking Nick's service to 30 to take that game, too. His returns were meticulously placed to cause Nick maximum discomfort as he scurried round the court. They never said much between points but if he'd been asked Denis would have admitted he'd probably never played better in his life. Every shot, including a wonderfully teasing lob that dropped millimetres inside the baseline, came off. He told himself he ought to have entered his club's senior tournament as well.

'You been having some private coaching from Pete Sampras or something?' Nick inquired peevishly when they paused for a necessary drink.

Denis shook his head. 'Just hitting form, I expect. Though, come to think of it, I'm not quite sure my timing's *quite* right just yet. I'll try and improve it a bit after I've won this first set 6–0.'

'You won't even win the next game,' Nick snorted. 'You were lucky to get a net cord in my first service game because that was the turning point! Otherwise . . .'

'Well, if you say so,' was the grinning, and thoroughly disbelieving, response. 'I'll concede this, buddy-buddy, maybe you weren't really concentrating, maybe you – '

'Nuts! I concentrate one hundred per cent on whatever I'm doing, you *know* that.' With commendable accuracy he tossed his drinks can into a distant litter-bin. 'Come on, I'll show you!'

But he didn't. Although he managed to win one game, the sixth, mainly as a result of a couple of service winners that Denis only just failed to return, the set slid easily away from him 1–6. He knew he couldn't put it down simply to Denis's brilliance because that was spasmodic. It was his own form that was so woeful and he couldn't see a reason.

One of the good things about Denis was that he didn't gloat. From his sports bag he produced a drinks cooler and then handed Nick another can. 'Go on, swig that down, it's full of energy. That's probably what you need to turn your form from sub-par to super-star – your usual performance, of course!'

'Thanks, Den. Look, I'm sorry I'm giving you a poor game. Point is, I'm probably on a bit of a low after that school match I told you about. I mean, I've just no idea what old Johnny Highton is going to do, whether I'm in or out of the team. If I'm out, well . . .'

Denis had never seen his friend so dispirited and couldn't believe that all his customary confidence had evaporated. Perhaps Nick needed a few sword thrusts to propel him back towards his ambitions. 'So are you thinking of quitting cricket, then? If so – '

'No way!' was the explosive reply. 'You know me better than that. This is just a, a hiccup. Listen, I'm going to have the longest Test career *ever*. I know exactly what I've got to beat. So how long d'you think the record is at present?'

Denis hadn't really wanted to divert into another cricket conversation, but he didn't object to the rest from the sweltering conditions on the court. Now that he was winning their match so easily he could afford to be sympathetic. 'Dunno – twenty years? That's a lifetime!'

'Thirty years and 315 days, that's the longest. Guy called Wilfred Rhodes, played for England and Yorkshire. Last played when he was aged fifty-two!'

'You won't be able to bowl fast for thirty years. You'll burn yourself out in half that time. Bound to.'

Nick considered that point of view. 'Well, maybe I'll turn to slow bowling – get it, *turn* to?' Denis's eyebrows merely went up as he closed his eyes and he didn't say a word, knowing Nick would continue. 'But just for the last couple of years. Then the selectors will see I'm the best slowie in the game and keep me on for

– what? – oh, another five years at least. That'll be it – record broken – and a new record that will *never* be beaten. So my name will always stay at the top of the list of all-time greats. Great!'

'You live in a fantasy land, you honestly do.'

'Well, just stick around and watch me prove you wrong.'

Denis laughed. 'Come on, you've had a long enough rest. Time for me to take the second set off you; 6–0 this time, I reckon.'

It wasn't. Nick, refreshed by the rest, played much better. His serve began to function more efficiently and he was willing to chase everything round the court. Denis, just as he usually did in the long run, began to make elementary mistakes. His stamina began to give out. Although he claimed to eat and drink energy foods, the truth was that he was too self-indulgent with the fattening snacks he couldn't resist. As he never had ambitions in sport to play for anything but fun, he claimed it didn't matter at all if he lost. But his best friend wasn't convinced of that.

The set reached a tie-break, a situation that revitalized both of them. Predictably, because of the power and accuracy of his serving, Denis won it – and, therefore, the match. Neither of them could contemplate another set in such heat. They were just about to leave the court when old John Stapleton, Arkenley's Life President and longest-serving supporter, paused by the gate to greet them.

'Not been making too much use of that right

shoulder of yours, have you, lad?' he inquired, looking at Nick.

'Er, no, I don't think so, Mr Stapleton,' he replied cautiously. 'Only had a couple of sets this morning.'

There was a nod of approval for that. 'You don't want to risk putting it out, you see. Can happen even at your age if you're not careful. With a bowling action like yours, young Nicholas, cricket must come first, you know.'

He must have noticed Denis's eyebrows rise for he added: 'He's good, this boy.'

Politely, Denis raised them again, saying: 'Oh, really? Now, why have I never heard that before from anyone else?'

Nick laughed and wished the old man a happy day. 'See you on Sunday – and I hope to give you something to cheer about, Mr Stapleton.'

'You do, son, you do. I'll be here, don't you doubt it.'

The day was getting better, that was what Nick didn't doubt at all. Although he could never forgive himself for losing at anything, even a friendly tennis joust with Denis, he was thrilled with the praise from John Stapleton, a man who had played at county level and was known to have a good eye for a promising player.

'Hope Dad's had a good morning and then he'll treat us to a really good lunch,' Denis remarked as they turned into the drive of the hotel where the auction was being held. 'I just fancy gammon, eggs and chips – oh, and they do a terrific sherry trifle here, too.'

'You can't be serious, even *you*, Den. You can't want to stuff yourself on a day like this!'

'Listen, mate, any day is a day to eat when the food's great. Anyway, don't suppose you'll starve yourself, will you?'

'I'll think about it. In fact, I've got plenty to think about. So . . .'

What dominated his thoughts was the forthcoming net practice at Trimdon School for the entire cricket squad. He knew he *must*, this time, make the best possible impression on Johnny Highton. If only the sports teacher could be persuaded to echo old Mr Stapleton's verdict. 'He's good, this boy.'

Four

From short range the ball came straight at him like an armour-piercing shell. Nick didn't move a millimetre. Taking the ball in his midriff he clutched it to himself, falling backwards in the same moment, falling so athletically he was able to complete a somersault before jumping high with the ball held aloft to celebrate the brilliance of the catch.

'That's quite enough, Freeland,' Mr Highton said tartly. 'We don't need histrionics like that.'

'I'm certainly not laughing, sir,' the fielder protested.

'Not hysterics, boy! Histrionics!' The frown deepened. 'Don't you understand simple English? Histrionics means – means play-acting. Being theatrical. We can do without that.'

He turned away to try and detect some flaw in a batsman's technique while Nick, throwing the ball back to one of the bowlers before waiting to perform in the nets, exchanged baffled glances with Lawrie Bellamey, the next-youngest member of the Trimdon first-team squad. Nick was wondering, but couldn't say, what he had to do next to attract the coach's attention and so persuade him that he ought to be allowed to have some bowling practice. After all, practically everybody else had had a go, including those who could only at best be described as occasional bowlers. So why was he being deliberately excluded?

Of course, he knew the reason: the notorious beamer in the Rochbury match, an incident that had become almost a legend within the school. In an inspired moment, Steven Lindley had described it as 'travelling like a guided missile with instructions to seek and destroy the batsman's head!' The sequel had been fairly predictable: Nick was awarded the soubriquet 'The Destroyer'. At first just amused by it, he now recognized that it might actually help his image as a fast bowler: in cricketing terms, the most destructive fast bowler the world had ever known, he hoped. But he wanted to be known for taking wickets, not terrorizing an opponent through a slip of the hand. And the only way he could achieve his immediate ambition was to win a regular place in the first XI. Unless he represented his school at senior level he had scarcely a hope of getting a chance to play in the county's youth team.

So far, in this session, he hadn't batted either, although Mr Highton's declared intention was to give everyone some practice 'because even if you're a complete rabbit the team may *need* runs from you to win a match'. All he'd done was field, and even his success there had come in for criticism, not praise. While he was reflecting on that, a skyer from a mis-hit by Steven soared almost vertically over the side-netting. Lawrie dashed forward to get under it, although probably nothing would have been said if the ball had been allowed to drop harmlessly to earth. Because it had gone so high Lawrie twice had to change position to be sure he was able to take it. Yet when it arrived at chest height he missed it completely.

'Sorry, lost it in the sun,' he explained cheerfully.

'Next time, hold your cap out,' Mr Highton remarked, grinning.

Nick couldn't believe such favouritism! Why should Lawrie's failure be excused with a joke when his own adhesive skills and athleticism were practically condemned? But he knew there was no point in complaining: Johnny Highton ran cricket school in his own way without reference to anyone apart from the boy he'd chosen to be captain.

Then, when Nick had just about given up hope of being directly involved in anything, Mr Highton picked up a ball and tossed it to him. 'Right, young Nicholas, your turn,' he announced. 'Do make sure, though, that the ball *bounces* before it reaches the batsman. Especially one on the short side like young Lawrie here.'

Nick kept silent and no one laughed audibly, for which he was thankful. Lawrie wasn't really small for his age, he merely looked rather slight because of his slimness and thin features. As a batsman it was his timing and the movement of his feet and wrists that had earned him such high regard from the perennially hard-to-please sports master. Already he had scored two 50s in successive matches against bowlers at least three or four years older than him, and he displayed no fear at all when the ball was flying round his ears. Indeed, nothing was more impressive than his playing of the hook shot.

Although Lawrie was facing a relay of other bowlers, Nick was sure that Mr Highton had deliberately pitted his two youngest squad members against one another to see which emerged on top. He would have worked out that they'd be determined to show off their best tricks. He was right. Nick's first delivery was as innocuous as could be and Lawrie came down the wicket to drive it past him at scorching speed all along the ground.

Nick, flaying himself for sending down such a tentative 'nothing' ball, daren't look at the coach; all too easily he could imagine his grim expression on noting the treatment it received. Gradually, however, he felt he was getting it right, keeping Lawrie on the back foot more often than not and then beating him with a choice away-swinger. The most frustrating part of the session, though, was having to wait to bowl because everyone had to take his turn. Then, after one longer wait than usual, Nick fired in a short ball. It didn't rise very high and for once Lawrie was unprepared. The ball struck him in the ribs and everyone within earshot heard the thump it made. The batsman dropped his bat and went down on his knees, doubled up.

Nick was the first to reach him. 'Sorry, Lawrie, sorry! Are you OK? I mean – '

Lawrie was always easily recognizable on the field because of the fairness of his hair. Now his face, beneath a light tan, was paler still. There were tears in his eyes, but quickly he brushed those away with the back of his hand.

Gently, Nick put his arm round him and encouraged him to stand, though Lawrie remained bent over, breathing heavily. The sports master, who'd been talking to Craig Gooding when the blow was struck, now dashed up and demonstrated equal compassion. Nick saw, thankfully, that colour was returning to Lawrie's face.

'How's it feel, Lawrence?' asked the coach, his fingers tenderly exploring the boy's rib-cage. 'You can breathe properly, can't you?'

'Yes – yes – I'm – I'm fine,' he gasped. 'Just – just winded. Shouldn't have missed – that ball.'

Mr Highton looked at Nick, who guessed he was about to receive another stinging comment on his bowling and probably the news that he was being taken off. He was wrong.

'Well, there was nothing wrong with that delivery – just short of a length. Well bowled, in fact,' the coach said calmly. 'Lawrence, you were a bit slow on to it, not like you at all. Anyway, is it getting easier?'

Lawrie straightened up at last, though he kept his left hand on the affected area. 'I think it's fine, now, sir. I don't want a break. I'm ready for the next ball.'

Mr Highton patted him on the shoulder in avuncular fashion. 'That's the spirit. If you fall off a horse, re-mount immediately. Then your nerve'll still be in place.'

Nick's spell of bowling had finished for the time being and as he waited his next turn Charlie Yorke sidled up to him. 'You always do that, go and chat up a batsman you've hit? Waste of time in my opinion. I mean, you've knocked him down, got him scared of you and then show you're *sorry*? Poor psychology.'

Nick shook his head. 'Don't agree. OK, I've scared him because he's been hit, but I want to get him out by good bowling, not terrorism. If I go and see how he is I actually probably get him to lower his guard for the next ball because he thinks I'm, well, a decent sort of guy. So maybe he won't expect a difficult ball next delivery. But I'll just fire 'em in in the same way, trying to get his wicket. And, as I say, maybe he's a bit relaxed because of my friendly attitude. Charlie, I swear, *I* don't go soft. But I believe there's nothing wrong with a bit of sympathy.'

Charlie shrugged. 'Oh well, it's up to you. We can't really tell now because Lawrie is getting all this bowling from everybody else. Anyway, it's your turn again.'

Lawrie had been coping manfully with a variety of bowling and displaying discomfort only occasionally by rubbing his side while waiting for the next ball. Nick, racing in, hit his chosen spot and saw the ball swing in at the batsman. Lawrie, treating a good delivery from N. Freeland with the same consideration he gave to everything he faced, dropped his hands and rendered it harmless. From his demeanour it was impossible to tell whether he was thinking about Nick's previous ball.

As a couple of bowlers dropped out after completing their stints Nick was able to start building up a real rhythm and his hope was that Lawrie would stay at the wicket and not be replaced. The batsman seemed to be less mobile than usual – perhaps that was one of the effects of the blow in the ribs. Whatever it was, Nick produced the ball he'd been striving for. Lawrie desperately jabbed down to try to keep it out but the ball skidded into the base of the stumps and knocked them askew.

Nick flung his arms up in triumph and Lawrie patted his bat to acknowledge the quality of the ball that had so comprehensively penetrated his defence. Eagerly, Nick swung round, full of hope that Mr Highton, too, was in a congratulatory mood. But he was out of luck there: the sports master was remonstrating with one of the opening batsmen who'd been fooling around, apparently trying to prove that his juggling skills with a football were just as effective when using a cricket ball. What the boy daren't admit was that he'd become bored since completing his own batting spell in the net.

Unfortunately, Nick had no chance to repeat Lawrie's dismissal because Mr Highton, resuming his scrutiny of the official training session, signalled that Lawrie should take a break, allowing Craig Gooding to have a bat. In a sense, that was to Nick's advantage: if he could bowl out the skipper a couple of times he'd surely have demonstrated that his bowling was too good to be ignored for the next match. Craig, however, seemed to be in imperious form and virtually nothing anyone sent down passed his bat. Nick was confident he might have got an lbw verdict in his favour on one occasion when he broke through. He suspected Mr Highton might not allow him to keep going much longer so he was putting everything he possessed into each delivery.

'Listen, can I give you a bit of advice?' Charlie said quietly as Nick retrieved a ball from a loose shot.

Surprised, Nick just nodded. He knew Charlie had been watching intently but hadn't imagined Trimdon's injured fast bowler had coaching aspirations.

'Well, it's this, you see. I've noticed you're still taking a very long run, just as far as you do in a match. But after four or five strides you sort of do a half-stride, a bit of a hiccup, really. Then you get going again. Nothing wrong with the last part of your run but I think you're wasting the first part, Nick.'

'Oh.' Nick didn't know what else to say because he certainly hadn't been aware of any interruption in his stride. In the past couple of years he'd spent a lot of time perfecting his run and thought it was as good as could be. Neither Mr Highton nor any of the senior players at Arkenley CC had mentioned any flaw.

'Look, I'm not trying to find fault for the sake of it,' Charlie added hastily, divining Nick's thoughts. 'Point is, *I* used to start too far back. I was wasting bags of effort without realizing it until a coach at another school spotted it and advised me to try a shorter run. The rhythm's a lot better since I changed. Hope you don't mind me telling you.'

'No, no, of course not, Charlie. I'll – er – give it a go, see what difference it makes to my action. Thanks.'

His first attempt to cut down his run didn't work at all, for he lost his stride completely, finishing up on the wrong foot and so was unable to release the ball. And it was just as bad when he tried again. When he wiped sweat from his forehead he knew it wasn't just his exertions in trying to bowl that had put it there.

'Doesn't seem to have worked,' he told Charlie, a hint of resentment in his voice.

Charlie shrugged. 'Not surprised. Takes time, you know, to change something as fundamental as that. You'll just have to work on it, Nick, if you want to.'

It had crossed Nick's mind that Charlie could have an ulterior motive for suggesting a change of run-up: after all, if Nick took his place in the Trimdon team and bowled brilliantly, Charlie himself might never get back into the side. But that seemed an unworthy thought and he knew he shouldn't pursue it. Instead, he asked Charlie how his injury was coming along.

'Slowly, I suspect. Still getting some throbbing under the splint.' He paused to scowl at it. 'They said to be patient. All right for them at *their* age. But I want to get on with my life.'

Nick was murmuring something sympathetic when he saw that Mr Highton was summoning the squad to gather round him. Perhaps it was the announcement of the team for the match against Winterton College. Instinctively, he crossed his fingers. *Surely* he would be selected . . .

'That was a good work-out, I'm pleased with you,' Mr Highton said. 'It's not easy at the end of a hard and hot day to put so much effort into bowling, so you did well, you speed merchants.'

Nick hoped he'd be mentioned by name but no one was; rather worryingly, the sports master didn't appear even to glance at him. With Charlie absent, there really wasn't anyone else who *could* be included. Unless – unless he played an extra batsman; Winterton's bowlers were reputedly very good indeed.

'So we'll be hoping for a repeat performance when we get into the real thing against Winterton,' Mr Highton went on. 'No slacking, everyone working hard as a steam engine. You don't win cricket matches by dozing on the edge of the boundary. Right, boys, I'm off. Keep fit and keep thinking cricket.'

That was often his farewell remark. The players all knew he had a theory that a team could, if it really put its mind to it, *think* out the opposition. Cricket, he insisted, was the thinking-man's game: if you applied your intelligence properly then you should be half-way to defeating the other team, however talented they might be. 'Guile and guts should be stuck together like bread and butter,' he'd once commented on a memorable occasion. 'A very satisfying combination.'

At that moment Nick's thinking revolved only around the composition of the team for the Winterton match. He recognized risks in asking the vital question, but couldn't resist it. 'Have you chosen the team, Mr Highton?' he inquired, in what he hoped was a nonchalant manner.

'I might have, and then again, I might wish to change my mind,' was the unhelpful reply. 'Best to mull these things over, not act impetuously. When people are impetuous it's often not to their advantage. I shall follow my usual practice and pin the team-sheet to the main notice-board at 10 o'clock tomorrow morning.'

Nick didn't need to ask who the sports master was referring to as impetuous: that was painfully obvious. Probably, he decided, he'd made a cardinal error in showing how desperate he was to learn his fate. Now he could do nothing but wait and see.

The hands of the art-room clock were moving with maddening slowness. Or they were as far as Nick Freeland was concerned that following morning. Every time he looked up the second hand had scarcely completed another revolution.

'Is there a time-bomb somewhere, ticking relentlessly away, that only you know about, Nicholas?' inquired Mr Vinsen, pleasantly enough.

'Er no, I don't think so, sir,' Nick replied feebly because he couldn't think of any better rejoinder to match the sarcasm.

'Ah, good. Well, now, perhaps you don't care all that much for designing posters for an advertising campaign. Strange, because you always strike me as an extrovert young man to whom self-promotion should have an instinctive appeal.'

Nick knew there was no sensible answer he could make to that point so he remained silent. Why was it, he wondered, that some teachers loved to show off their verbal skills when it must be obvious to them that the person they were talking to was simply trying to wrestle with a problem? There was no answer to that, either. His eyes strayed to the clock yet again: 10.06. Surely the team-sheet was in place by now. Mr Highton was a stickler for punctuality.

This time Mr Vinsen's tone was sharper and accompanied by a sigh of exasperation. 'Look, Nicholas, if this topic is so utterly boring to you that you can't wait to get out, go now. Go on, feel free to go. Just so long as you call at the Headmaster's office on the way to wherever you're going.'

So he could get out! He hadn't thought it would be so easy. But *some* subtlety was needed for them both to keep face. 'Well, it's my stomach, you see, Mr Vinsen. Churning round and round. I was wondering if I could survive until the bell goes. But, well, I think I'd better be safe and go now. You know, to the loo. Can't think what I ate . . .'

'Off you go then.'

Luckily, the toilets were in the same corridor as the notice-board and, deliberately, he made himself call in en route, just for luck and to give Mr Highton another few moments, if he needed them, to post the team-sheet.

And there it was: placed absolutely in the centre of the section headed 'Sports Notices': *School's First Eleven v. Winterton College (away)*. First: *C. Gooding (capt.)* and finally: *N. Freeland*.

He was in!

He might, at that moment, have literally jumped for joy if he hadn't seen, approaching slowly, hands behind his back in classical headmasterly pose, the unmistakable figure of Hugh Rossiter, popularly known as Ross the Boss.

'Taking a little breather from lessons, are you, Nicholas?' the Head inquired with his customary smile.

'Had to go to the loo, sir, and then I couldn't miss the chance of seeing who's in the team against Winterton.'

'And is your name in the list?'

'Yes, yes it is. Great, isn't it?'

He hadn't meant to say that, but couldn't hold back his pleasure. In any case, Mr Rossiter's smile encouraged enthusiastic responses; the only time to worry with him was when he wasn't smiling. Nicholas liked the fact that he didn't have to look up at the Headmaster: they were almost identical in height. For that reason alone, he felt he could always get on with him.

'I'm pleased that you're pleased,' the Boss went on,

smile still in place and his fingers straying to caress his trim moustache for probably the hundredth time that day. 'I'm sure your keenness will be rewarded – perhaps a century?'

'I'm best at bowling, sir. Actually, I want to play cricket more than anything else in life. I want to be, I'm *going* to be, the fastest bowler in the world.'

Mr Rossiter's expression didn't change at all as he took in what Nick immediately recognized as a ridiculous boast; it would be all right saying that to a mate, but not to your Headmaster before you'd even established a place in the school team, let alone played for a county youth side. Yet he really believed it would be true one day.

'Good, good, self-belief like yours is to be admired,' the Boss told him. 'If you're going to be as good as that, I'd better come and see you in action before some other leading team snaps you up and I've missed my chance. Just one word of caution, though, Nicholas: don't neglect your academic studies. You'll almost certainly still need a worthwhile career when your cricketing days are over. Sport doesn't last a lifetime, not even for the most gifted performers. Understood?'

'Yes, sir – and thank you.'

Nick took the hint and raced back up the stairs to the art room.

Five

The weather had broken at last. Nick heard the rain against the windows when he awoke that morning and couldn't believe he was going to be so unlucky. Why did things have to go wrong on the day he was to play in the most important cricket match of his life?

It was distinctly discouraging when he yanked aside the curtains to see water streaming down the glass and ominously dark clouds apparently stationary above the neighbourhood. The previous days had been as brilliant as any for the past couple of weeks with no hint of squalls.

'Oh yes there was,' his mother contradicted him when he complainingly came down to breakfast. 'The TV weatherman got it absolutely right last night. They usually do, these days: those satellites up there have transformed meteorological predictions into a real science. I'm surprised they haven't told you that at school.'

'All right, then, if they know so much, what's going to happen later on?' countered Nick as he bit into a bacon sandwich. His mother preferred him to eat fruit and fibre but she indulged him in his favourite breakfast food on special occasions. 'You obviously listened to every word of the forecast.'

'The storms will have blown themselves out by mid-morning, clouds will clear, the sun will come out and the temperature rise. You should find the rain will have freshened up the wicket nicely for your sort of pace. So you'd better keep your fingers crossed that Trimdon win the toss and decide to put Winterton in to bat. Or, if Winterton win the toss, they misread the signs and decide to bat first.'

'Good thinking,' exclaimed Nick, cheering up instantly. Though he found it hard to admit as much to anyone, his mother was usually right about most things. His faith in her cricketing knowledge and skills was unbounded. But most of the players he mixed with wouldn't believe that any female could be an authority on the game, let alone have played it at national level. So he scarcely ever mentioned the significant part she played in his sporting life.

Just as she predicted, the weather improved radically through the morning and, as Winterton was only a couple of miles away on the other side of the town, no one had doubts about prospects for play. They travelled in a convoy of cars and Johnny Highton himself was the chauffeur for Nick, Steven Lindley and Jack Songhurst, the wicketkeeper.

To Nick's surprise the chief topic of conversation was a television programme the other two boys had watched the previous evening; and even the sports master joined in as it turned out he'd been intending to see the same programme but missed it. None of them seemed to be the slightest bit interested in discussing the match that was about to be played. Perhaps, though, that was a superstition among regular first XI players: it might be bad luck to try to anticipate what would happen. All the same, Nick was keen to know whether he was going to open the bowling with Adam Lexton, Charlie Yorke's customary partner. It would be a huge disappointment to be relegated to the role of first-change bowler (it couldn't be worse than that because no one else in the team possessed any pace at all).

'What d'you think our chances are, sir?' Nick couldn't refrain from asking their leader when they collected their kit from the boot of the car in the park that overlooked the beautiful oval of Winterton's cricket field. Trees lined three sides of the ground and on the fourth side, where the black-and-white pavilion stood, the view was of distant gentle hills.

'Could depend on which side wins the toss,' was the cautious reply. 'The rain should have livened up the pitch, unless it's been covered. And I don't imagine they'd think to do that last night after the weather we've been having.'

'Should suit you, then, Destroyer!' remarked Jack, looking at Nick and grinning.

Nick didn't need to say anything. He wondered whether the new nickname would stick: he was quite happy to accept it so long as it wasn't reduced to Des, which sounded awful to him.

'Listen, if I win the toss we'll field,' Craig Gooding murmured to Nick as they all descended the steps to the cricket ground. 'I'll let you have the new ball, so make sure you don't waste it, OK?'

'Certainly won't, Skipper,' Nick, thoroughly relieved by that news, responded.

Craig dumped his bag in the pavilion and then went off with his opposite number, Carl Waterfield, for the ritual inspection of the pitch. He and Carl, known to everyone at his school as Meadow, or Med for short, tossed up.

'He won it – but he's chosen to bat!' Craig, rubbing his hands with glee and eager anticipation of the outcome, reported to his team. 'Maybe he thinks our bowling's weak without Charlie. So, young Nick, you show 'em they've miscalculated!'

Nick had thought about this moment, and planned for it, for a long time. All his ambitions for his future in cricket might be affected by what happened to him in this match. Although he'd often thought vaguely in such terms in previous, minor, games he was absolutely sure that this match against Winterton could change his life. He *had* to make a major impact on everyone who was taking part or simply watching. There was no sign at this stage of Ross the Boss, but he recognized it was unlikely that Trimdon's Head would be here this early even if he turned up at all. In any case, Mr Rossiter probably had little real interest in Nick Freeland's sporting future.

'Looks a bit greener than I'd expected,' remarked Jack Songhurst to Nick as they studied the pitch. 'Should speed things up a bit for you.'

'Hope so. I'm going flat out from the start. So, Jack, don't try to stand up too close to the stumps, OK? Any snicks'll probably carry for miles!'

He grinned as he said that although he was hoping the wicketkeeper would take the comment seriously. Jack was inclined to do things his own way and he might want to indicate that he didn't think his opening bowler was all that fast.

Nick was also at the mercy of his captain, who tended to make field placings without wasting time consulting the bowler about his preferences. On the other hand, Craig was shrewd in making changes once the match was in progress and he'd seen how the opposition were playing their shots and which areas they favoured. So Nick guessed it was up to himself to demonstrate immediately what he could achieve on this probably quite lively wicket.

His one dilemma concerned his run-up; should he revert to his original twenty-two strides or bowl off the shortened distance that had eventually proved so effective for Charlie Yorke? Of course, he could switch from one to the other if necessary, but maintaining his rhythm mattered more than anything. Even as he began to mark out his run he hadn't finally decided what to do.

Then, almost as if he'd received a message through thought transference, he glanced up to see Charlie Yorke standing on the boundary edge and holding up his thumb in a 'good luck' gesture. Nick nodded to show his appreciation and dragged his toe across the turf to remind himself of the starting point of the shorter run. The ball was tossed to him by Tris Morton, stationed at mid-off, and he examined it carefully, even to the extent of rubbing away with his thumb at an imaginary imperfection in the leather. His heartbeat settled down again to normality as he turned sharply and began to race towards the stumps when the umpire signalled that play should begin.

In the split-second he reached his delivery stride and his arm came over, Nick knew everything was going to be just right. The ball pitched a fraction short of a length, appeared to hold its course, then swung sharply under a bat that was describing a sort of vague arc – and flattened the off-stump.

The batsman stared, transfixed, at the damage as if he couldn't believe his eyes. Craig, standing just a metre or so back from the stumps at first slip, flung his arms into the air with similar disbelief, but in his case mixed with barely expressible delight. For the first time anyone could remember he actually trotted down the wicket to congratulate the bowler. Both Tris and Blake Carberry, a middle-order batsman, beat him to it: and Nick was suddenly overwhelmed with congratulations of a kind he hadn't experienced before at school.

It was, he knew, perhaps the best ball he'd bowled; certainly it was his best first ball of an opening spell in any match. He contentedly accepted the plaudits, the back-slapping, the handshakes, the euphoria that the removal of that single stump created.

'*Really* moved off the pitch, Nick,' the skipper told him, only marginally devaluing the delivery. 'So keep on pitching 'em up and we'll carve through 'em like a knife through butter.'

It wasn't an original simile and exaggeration of that kind was unlike him. Nick, though, was delighted, for it showed for the first time that he'd really been accepted into the school's first XI. He swung round to search for Charlie; he didn't have to look far. The disabled fast bowler was standing in the same spot and his thumb was raised again.

'If I can do it once, I can do it again – do it, do it, DO IT!' Nick told himself with fierce urgency as he hurried back to his mark with the new batsman at the crease. The wicket hadn't been a fluke and no one thought it was, least of all those fielders who'd seen it close up (the victim, of course, hadn't seen it at all, only the result). Craig had seen the help afforded by the pitch, but he remained in precisely the same spot at slip for the next ball. So did the wicketkeeper. Nick thought they were both far too close to the stumps, but decided to keep his thoughts to himself.

With the same smooth acceleration, Nick came up to the wicket, his arm almost brushing against the umpire as he fired the next lethal delivery. This time the tall, broad-shouldered batsman took half a step forward, attempted to jab down on the ball to anaesthetize the danger – and got a top edge. The ball flew high over his shoulder and even higher over Jack Songhurst and couldn't be stopped by anyone before it thudded loudly into the base of a tree beyond the boundary.

This time Nick's hands flew high above his head in despair. If only Jack Songhurst had done as he'd asked him before the match started it would have been two wickets in two balls. If he'd been standing back he'd have caught it comfortably. Instead, his immobility had failed everyone in the team, not just the bowler.

There were signals of 'bad luck' from 'keeper and captain and second slip and Nick had to try and look philosophical, knowing that Johnny Highton would be watching his every move and gesture. His one consolation was that he'd bowled another superb ball which the batsman couldn't fail to know he was lucky to survive. Carl Waterfield, due in next, and the rest of the Winterton team sprawled in and around the pavilion must surely be wondering how they were going to cope with Nicholas Freeland.

Somehow the batsman failed to get a touch to the third ball of the over, which whistled into Jack's grasp. He missed the next ball as well, blocked the fifth – and was plumb lbw to the last. His expression as he departed was one almost of relief rather than dismay at getting out. He knew he was lucky to have four runs to his name.

Nick's elation was matched by the rest of the Trimdon team as they moved into new positions for Adam Lexton's first over.

'Great stuff, Nick!' the skipper approved, while Jack, walking beside him, said: 'Sorry about the one that went over my head. Never had a hope of getting a glove on it!'

'Well, maybe you could move back a bit for my next over,' Nick suggested. 'I may be getting a bit faster now.'

Jack and Craig exchanged glances but neither spoke, so Nick had no idea whether he'd said the right thing or not. Still, *he* was the one who'd taken the wickets with bowling that was fast and menacing and right on target. Nobody could argue about that. Already he'd put Trimdon in a powerful position to win the match and it was only one over old.

The skipper set an attacking field for Adam. Nick, who hoped he might be rewarded with a place closer to the wicket, was sent to long on where there might be plenty of work if Adam strayed down the leg side; or bowled short. In fact, Adam found a length immediately and kept the pressure on. All the batsmen could manage were a couple of fairly streaky singles while Adam had a deafening appeal for caught-behind turned down.

Nick took the ball again eagerly for his second over. If he could break through again Trimdon would be completely in the driving seat unless things went drastically wrong. It was disappointing to see, though, that Jack Songhurst hadn't moved back so much as a millimetre. All Nick could hope was that the next snick, and there were bound to be a few, would go unerringly into his gloves. And stay there. On the other hand, the best thing Nick could do would be to hit the stumps without help from anyone.

The brief interlude in the field hadn't spoiled Nick's accuracy or his confidence in his new approach to the wicket. Once again he forced the batsman to play every ball. Nick's attempt at a yorker didn't come off but the batsman, unnerved by his failure to cope with this bowler, succeeded only in blocking the ball. Off the fifth he tore out of the straight-jacket by thrashing a good length ball past mid-off and streaking to the other end; when he saw that his partner wasn't content to take strike the single turned into a two. The batsman faced Nick's final ball of the over with renewed confidence. He had obviously decided that the best way to play this bowler was to take him on, show him who was in charge.

He took a step down the wicket to drive the next, well-pitched delivery, swung, got an inside edge and heard the fateful noise of his stumps being destroyed. He crashed his bat against his pad and then the ground at suffering what *he* knew was the worst luck in the world.

Nick knew that *his* luck was still in; it wasn't a bad ball, but it hadn't deserved a wicket. Still, the batsman had been generally fortunate to survive the earlier part of the over so he could hardly complain. And Nick rejoiced. Three wickets for six runs in twelve balls!

This time half the team seemed to charge towards him to celebrate the latest success, even Craig breaking into a run so as not to be the last to slap him on the back.

'Great stuff,' the captain said again. 'They're on the ropes now, groggy and reeling. So just keep delivering, Nick, and they'll be knocked out for good in no time.'

It was the first time Nick had heard his skipper say so much. The boxing metaphors also revealed a side of him he hadn't known about.

'I was a bit lucky really because that ball was a bit off-line – it was a good job he got that inside edge,' he admitted.

Jack, perhaps trying to make up for his own touch of ill-fortune (as he thought of it), denied that immediately. 'Oh, no, Nick, don't say that! You were right on line there, mate. He was lucky to get a bat on it!'

There was no point in arguing about it. Nick had something else on his mind. 'Skipper, d'you think we could have a third slip or a closer gully? I mean, with the ball swinging like it is I could get a few more top edges.'

Craig frowned. 'Don't know about that.' Quickly he looked round and apparently saw what he expected to see. 'Thought so. Med Waterfield's coming in next. Must've been holding himself back because of early wickets. He's strong on the leg side, gets nearly all his runs there. So I should be strengthening the on side, not the off. We'll see.'

Nick had to be content with that. It surprised him that Craig knew so much about Winterton's skipper, though he supposed, on reflection, that the pair of them must have played against each other in the past. It hadn't occurred to him that Craig was such an observant type, for he gave the impression that his style of captaincy relied simply on responding to events on the field, not shaping them.

As he returned to his fielding position at long on, Nick pondered on the subject of captains. Why were so many of them batsmen? He'd followed cricket, and read its history, for a long time so he knew about national leaders like Atherton and Gooch and Gower of England and Mark Taylor and Border of Australia, all of them batsmen. Ian Botham (England) and Imran Khan (Pakistan) were leading wicket-takers but then they were also run-makers with centuries to their names, so they'd be classed as all-rounders. The only out-and-out opening bowler he could think of who'd captained England was Bob Willis. That hardly seemed fair. Bowlers were just as important as batters: so why weren't they regarded as prospective leaders, too?

There was no time to pursue that subject further at present. Carl Waterfield was on strike and his first scoring shot was heading straight for long on, exactly as Craig might have predicted. Nick raced to it, swooped and threw it while still on the run, a throw so accurate that the wicketkeeper didn't have to move to take it. There was applause for the fielder from spectators as well as from captain and 'keeper. Nick's star was still in the ascendancy but it was to be his last success for a few overs.

Carl Waterfield had plainly decided to play a captain's role, mixing caution with occasional aggression but really taking no chances at all of losing his wicket through rashness. His partner, too, seemed to gain confidence in his company and together they staged a recovery for Winterton. The shell-shocked home supporters at last began to clap every scoring stroke and cheer each boundary.

Adam, beginning to lose his length, was replaced by Blake Carberry, more a batsman than a bowler but capable of surprising batsmen with cutters that deviated sharply. Unfortunately, those deliveries were produced out of the hat only occasionally; his stock ball tended to sit up and beg to be hit. And Carl was getting into the mood to hit them as far and as hard and as frequently as possible. So Craig removed Blake from the firing line, replacing him with Tristan Morton. Nick bowled unchanged at the other end.

Nick was beginning to tire, though he'd be loath to admit it. The sun was now quite strong and he was no longer getting movement off the pitch, it having dried out completely. Although both batsmen were still treating him warily, he was no longer constantly forcing them on to the defensive. Craig had started to push fielders back and second slip had vanished. Between overs Nick mentioned that to Charlie Yorke, who'd come round for a chat.

'Well, you could ask for him back, but I don't think Craig will play ball there,' Charlie remarked. 'He always prefers his own field placings, so you have to nudge him into changes in such a way he doesn't seem to be giving in to you.'

That was altogether too devious for Nick to contemplate, let alone attempt, at this stage of a match. Moreover, he didn't really want to risk losing Craig's support now that he'd demonstrated he thoroughly deserved to be in the team. So he would have to soldier on, to use one of Denis Demarco's favourite expressions.

As it turned out, his military spell lasted only one more over. Tempting fate for once, Carl flashed, and flashed very hard indeed, at his final delivery, getting a thinnish edge. The ball positively rocketed to the boundary, straight through the gap where second slip had stood. Nick's back arched and his hands went back in despair. Somehow he managed not to utter an audible sound: the curses were swallowed.

'Hard luck – but well bowled, Nick,' Craig told him as they met half-way down the wicket. 'I'll give you a break now. Have a go myself. Maybe the change of pace'll work!'

It may have been that, or something entirely different, but within a couple of overs Winterton had lost two more wickets, including that of their newly attacking captain. He was the first to go when, after playing a forceful shot against a fairly innocuous ball from Craig, he called for a run behind square leg. But Blake, the fielder, turned and picked up in the same movement and aimed for the stumps. Carl's partner, seeing the danger, yelled 'No!' and scrambled back to safety at his own end while Carl had to slither to a halt, try to turn and make his ground. He really hadn't any hope at all. With a very rueful look at his partner, he departed for the pavilion.

Perhaps unnerved by the experience of helping to contribute to his skipper's downfall, his ex-partner was the next to go. Tris Morton unexpectedly got a well-flighted ball to lift in the following over; the Winterton player didn't know how to deal with it and, trying to flick it away, succeeded only in giving a simple catch to the wicketkeeper. Jack, of course, had been standing up to Tris's gentle bowling and he enjoyed the triumph as much as the bowler did. But then, Tris wasn't a regular wicket-taker at this level, he, too, having only recently got into the side.

At 61 for 5, Winterton were really struggling and Nick wondered whether, with two new batsmen at the crease, he would be called back into the attack. But if that idea had occurred to Craig he certainly didn't act on it. The newcomers were allowed to play themselves in against moderate bowling. Runs were starting to flow again until one well-rounded batsman seemed to have a rush of blood to the head. Advancing down the pitch, he swung heartily against Tris's spin, missed the ball completely and was comprehensively stumped by the jubilant Jack. If anything, Tris appeared still more delighted and almost on the verge of turning cartwheels. With Johnny Highton still a figure of solemn concentration in front of the pavilion it was just as well Tris resisted his wildest celebratory urges.

Yet another wicket fell quickly before a stubborn

stand developed between Winterton's wicketkeeper and their youngest player, an all-rounder making his debut and clearly determined to mark it with a good score to his name. Craig, seemingly in the belief that they couldn't really last long, persisted with his own and Tris's bowling until Steven Lindley whispered something to him at the end of an expensive over. The skipper appeared to mull it over, then nodded, half to himself, and summoned Nick to have a word with him.

'Listen, we've got to break this stand,' he murmured, stating the obvious. 'I need you to go flat out, banging in a few short ones if you like. Next over I'll bring Adam back at the other end. The pace of the pair of you should sort 'em out.'

Six

Nick smiled his approval of getting the ball again, began vigorously rubbing it down the seam of his trousers and strode off to his mark. He was pleased the skipper hadn't suggested that he change ends, for he had never cared for that ploy. Once he'd got wickets he never wanted to switch to the other end, partly because he feared his luck might change. But with Craig, one never knew what tactic he might try next.

His first ball was a loose half-volley which, he couldn't deny, got the treatment it deserved; after that he returned to his familiar and effective line-and-length groove. With overs running out, as well as wickets, Winterton had to go for runs or get out. They managed both. Their wicketkeeper really chanced his arm, aiming to slog anything at all that was even marginally short of a length, and the fates seemed to be on his side – for three overs, anyway. Adam mortifyingly dropped a catch off his own bowling, the batsman survived a hairsbreadth decision over a probable run-out, and then Adam suffered again when he clean bowled his opponent only to be told it was a no-ball.

It was Nick who collected his wicket after producing a short, rising ball that sent the umpire's eyebrows in the same direction. The batsman fended the ball off without giving a catch or getting a run. Relieved to find that the next ball wasn't nearly so dangerous-looking, he tried to hit it out of the ground. Thoughtlessly, he didn't move his feet at all, so when he failed to make contact the umpire had the easiest decision of the day to give him out lbw. The following over he struck again, this time knocking the middle and leg stumps askew when the newcomer, Winterton's fastest bowler, went for glory without even keeping his eye on the ball.

Nick clenched his fists in glee. Five wickets! It was the mark by which bowlers were measured and he'd achieved it the first time he'd been given the new ball in a school match. Almost as soon as the applause broke out he shot a glance at the sports master to see whether he was joining in: and he was, calmly, politely, plainly not excited by that wicket or the overall haul, but clapping none the less. It surely meant that Nick Freeland was in favour.

But, to his chagrin, the Winterton tail continued to wag. The No. 11 poked about or defended dourly while, at the other end, the debutant hit about him carefully and lustily, even scoring successive fours off two of Nick's deliveries that were only fractionally off line. Nick retaliated with a short ball that the batsman fended off with his shoulder, the ball landing harmlessly wide of the stumps.

Because he didn't give any indication that he was in pain, Nick didn't go down the wicket to ask him if he was all right. If the youngster wanted to play the hard man, so be it. What annoyed him most was that his average was being damaged; and, what's more, the Winterton total was now a good deal higher than it ought to have been.

Craig decided something had to be done about this increasingly irritating last-wicket stand. He took Adam off and seized the ball himself. It might have been the complete change of pace that undid the No. 11, for, deciding to hit out at last, he mis-timed the shot and merely spooned the easiest of catches to the bowler.

'Should never have taken myself off in the first place,' the captain said when Nick congratulated him on his success. It was impossible to tell whether he meant it or was making a joke. Nick thought that, on balance, it had to be the former.

'A total of 133 is a lot more than it should have been,' was Mr Highton's greeting as his team came off the field. 'You let them off the hook after they were five down for less than half that.'

Then he turned with a less-severe expression to the opening bowler. 'But you, young Nicholas, bowled very well, very well indeed. Intelligently and fast. Can't ask more than that, can we?'

Nick hardly knew what to say. He'd hoped for praise, but nothing so extravagant as this from someone who usually was inclined to say little in the way of approval. 'Er, thanks, sir. I think getting somebody out with the first ball helped a lot, gave me bags of confidence.'

'Ah, yes, confidence; that's what we all need, for just about everything in life,' was the philosophical response. 'If we have confidence we can do almost anything. And if you carry on in this confident vein, well, Master Yorke may find it difficult to get his place back!'

Adam Lexton, who'd been hovering within ear-shot in the hope of picking up some personal crumbs from the boss man's table, positively beamed. If that meant what he thought it must mean then his own performance as an opening bowler was at least satisfactory and so *he* wouldn't be dropped to make way for the return of Charlie Yorke. Perhaps Mr Highton had completely overlooked the spilled chance off his own bowling. Really, he should have known better.

'You could've pitched 'em up a bit more, Adam,' the sports master said in a sad tone. 'You let them score much too freely when the main thing was to contain them after that early breakthrough. It's a cardinal error to drop a catch at any time, but when you do it off your own bowling, well, you might as well have shot yourself in the foot *and* injured your team-mates in the blast at the same time.'

He smiled thinly as if he wasn't entirely pleased with that analogy and then turned away to discuss the plan for the rest of the game with Craig and the opening batsmen.

'Come on, Nick, I need a lie down after that!' Adam exclaimed in mock horror. 'I get the feeling that if we lose this game I'll be the one to blame. Honestly, you can't win with old Highbrow. Well, maybe *you* can.'

They took their drinks out on to the banking where they could lie full-length, hands behind their heads, to watch the progress of the game. Watching the start of his team's innings when he knew he'd bowled well was always a time to enjoy life, in Nick's view.

He was soon sitting bolt upright, eyes wide open, watching in dismay as Trimdon's opening bat trudged back towards the pavilion, not a run on the scoreboard and one wicket down. The start of their innings was just as disastrous as Winterton's, with calamity in the first over as Timothy Thomson, known to all as Timbo, swung recklessly at the fifth ball from an energetic, tall bowler with a strange windmilling action, somehow contriving to send it up to low-cloud height and then watching as the wicketkeeper gratefully received it.

'Must have moved miles off its line,' Timbo muttered unconvincingly to anyone who'd listen as he slumped on to a rustic seat to take off his pads.

Timbo's downfall was duplicated in the very next over when his fellow opener, desperate to see some runs on the board, drove too soon at a good-length ball to provide mid-off with a comfortable catch. Winterton's players were ecstatic and the soccer-style celebrations caused the umpire to tell their captain to calm things down.

'Oh, no!' Adam groaned, while Nick cast an interested glance at Mr Highton to see how he was reacting. But the coach had his eyes closed and his face was expressionless. Perhaps, Nick decided, that was because the whole scene was just too awful to contemplate.

'If this goes on, you and I will have to rescue us with the *bat*,' Adam said. Like most fast bowlers, he believed his batting was undervalued and that his place should be higher in the order. He was certain he could cope in a crisis that demanded runs from a last-wicket partnership. No, not just cope, *flourish*.

'Well, I don't mind, this pitch is great for batting now,' replied Nick, sipping at a mango-and-pineapple concoction. 'In fact, I really fancy having a bat. Could be my lucky day all round.'

However, it looked for a time as though Craig, who'd gone in to join Steven, had steadied the ship he commanded. The Windmill, whose real name was Jake Sango, was tending to spray the ball around as he strove to bowl ever faster. Steven could feast on that sort of diet for days at a time and after he'd hit four boundaries in the space of two overs his captain took the Windmill off. As it turned out, that was an inspired move, for the replacement bowler deceived Craig with his flight and turn. Craig was so surprised he made the elementary error of not regaining his crease after missing the ball and so was neatly stumped. This time, Johnny Highton's expression could only be described as bleak. Sensibly, Trimdon's skipper didn't say a word to him as he stalked past into the pavilion.

Blake Carberry, who was in next, responded to the off-spinner's enthusiasm by treating every ball as if it were lethal, even when it was short of a length and well wide of the stumps. He gave the impression that, whatever he might fail to do, he was going to stay out in the middle.

'Oh, come on!' Adam urged when another innocuous ball was allowed to escape any kind of punishment. 'Hit out or get out! This is a limited-overs match, you know, not a five-day Test!'

Blake couldn't possibly have heard him, but even if he had it wouldn't have made any difference; he continued to drop his hands or pad the ball away or, increasingly, avoid playing any shot whatsoever. Steven, meanwhile, was picking his targets judiciously and scoring well. It didn't seem to occur to him that a word with his partner might be helpful in an effort to raise the run-rate. Steven, like some other highly motivated batsmen, tended to live in his own world and thus be concerned only with his own performance at the crease.

Then Winterton introduced into their attack a player with a bowling action even more eccentric than the Wind-mill's: just as he was reaching the stumps his right arm disappeared behind his back, stretching almost to his left armpit before reappearing with such momentum that he almost swung himself off his feet as he released the ball. The oddity of this approach seemed to unnerve Blake, who should have been watching his partner on strike and not allowing himself to be mesmerized by the bowler's style. And it was that lack of concentration that cost Trimdon their best batsman.

Steven played a forceful shot well wide of mid-on and yelled 'Yes!' He was into his stride immediately but Blake was still so bemused by what he'd been watching that he didn't move at all. Then, when he saw what was happening, that the fielder had now reached the ball, he belatedly replied 'No! No!' And Steven, relying on ancient instincts instead of continuing his run, turned as fast as he could, stumbled, recovered his balance but failed to regain his crease by practically a metre before the 'keeper triumphantly swept off the bails. Trimdon were now 40 for 4.

'Oh, no! The clown!' Adam cried.

'Who – oh, you mean Blake, of course,' Nick remarked. 'Bet old Steven is using stronger language than that.'

He was. But he wasn't saying anything at all as he stomped up the steps into the dressing-room. Mr Highton hadn't detained him for he was having a quick word with Nick, much to Nick's surprise.

'If Songhurst also perishes as a result of some foolhardy play or also displays suicidal tendencies then you'll be in next,' he declared. 'And I want you to show some responsibility and common sense. Understood?'

'Er, yes, sure, Mr Highton,' Nick replied. He was still surprised to be getting this sort of instruction. Did it mean that the sports master *was* treating him as an all-rounder rather than as a bowler who could bat a bit when necessary? After all, he was being promoted in the order.

'If Carberry and Songhurst can carry on for a bit and boost the total, well, we can still win this one – and I most definitely don't want to lose to Winterton. They really aren't up to our level so I don't want them getting above themselves with a false victory.'

Until he heard that declaration Nick hadn't realized just how keen, in a personal sense, the sports master was to win this match. No wonder he was pleased with Nick's bowling; if he could find similar praise for his batting, well, his future in the team was assured. He almost began to wish that one of the pair at the crease *would* get out so that Nick himself would have a chance of glory with the bat. But he didn't expect that wish to be granted as quickly as the next over while Nick was strapping on his pads in leisurely fashion.

Songhurst, clearly imbued with the 'let's-get-on-with-it' spirit that Blake just as plainly lacked, jumped out to drive a ball short of a length, missed it badly and had his stumps wrecked by his fellow wicketkeeper. He had every reason to turn round and view the demolition site with mortification. He could scarcely have played his stroke in worse fashion.

Nick gulped, grabbed his bat and got a cheerful 'Go for it!' from Adam who would never have admitted he was secretly hoping to join him at the wicket. Swinging his bat round and round to give himself extra confidence and to show the opposition that he meant business, Nick reached the middle where Blake wanted a private word.

'Watch out,' he warned. 'They're sending down

some good stuff. That spinner can be hard to read.'

Nick just nodded. Although plenty of overs remained Trimdon, at 44 for 5, needed runs soon if they were to overhaul Winterton's total. On the other hand, he would have to take a look at the bowling, and work out where he should be hitting the ball.

The first ball he received was so wide it could have been signalled as such, but Nick wasn't going to miss a scoring chance like that. Moving out to it nimbly, he drove it square to the boundary. It gave him enormous satisfaction to get off the mark with a four. A few more loose deliveries like that and he could look forward to an exciting innings. A glance to the other end, however, revealed the pained expression on Blake's face. Plainly Nick's partner didn't approve of such rapid scoring! Nick guessed that probably there'd be a warning from Blake at the end of the over not to rush things. There was. By then, though, Nick had not only brought up the 50 for Trimdon but reached double figures himself. With the bowler straying down the leg side, Nick pulled the ball wide of square leg and next ball hammered his shot in the direction of an indolent mid-on. When the fielder woke up, the batsmen had sprinted the first run and were cantering the second.

He felt fired up. Everything was going miraculously well. The bowling really was very, very ordinary; at least, this off-spinner was. Nick had taken wickets and his eye was in and Johnny Highton had praised him and believed his batting was good enough to move him up the order. The wicket, he suspected, was playing much more easily than when Trimdon had been bowling. There really was no reason why they couldn't win this match. He ought to tell Blake, the senior batsman, just to keep his end up and let Nick Freeland get the runs! But he didn't.

Blake treated the medium pace at the other end with his usual caution although, so far as he could tell, Nick was sure it wasn't troublesome stuff. By body language he hoped to let Blake know he was ready to run the fastest single if necessary; but memories of what happened the last time he backed up too far still haunted him. Nothing would be worse than losing his wicket in such idiotic fashion.

Blake, for his part, did manage to pinch a couple of easy singles and got a streaky two down to third man. If they could keep up a rate of four runs an over then victory would be theirs. The round-faced off-spinner with beefy forearms rolled in for his next over and, once again, Nick launched himself into the attack, driving, pulling and then, to his delight, chopping him down behind point with such exquisite timing that third man had no hope of cutting off the boundary. In two overs Nick himself had registered 20 and Trimdon were now 68 for 5, more than half-way to the total needed to win the match. Not once had Nick felt the slightest doubt about how to play any ball he received: he'd simply dealt with each on its merits. And, in doing so, he was enjoying himself hugely. Cricket, he could tell himself, was sometimes a very simple game.

His batting partner didn't think so. Somehow he

managed to avoid playing-on the best ball he received, survived an appeal for lbw by a narrow margin and then clipped a two off his legs for his only scoring stroke of the over. Still, looking at the scoreboard, which was updated at the end of every over and supplied only basic information, he could take pleasure in the thought that the Trimdon score was now a healthy 70.

To no one's surprise, Jake Sango, the Windmill, was brought back to replace the toothless off-spinner and curb Trimdon's dashing all-rounder. Nick twirled his bat and awaited the first delivery, which he supposed might be a bouncer. It was. His first thought was to try to hook it, his second to duck. Although the frantic Windmill had put his heart into getting the ball to bounce it hadn't really risen as high as he'd hoped. Nick barely felt it, though the ball flicked against the top of his shoulder before skidding away past leg slip. Because he wasn't sure where it had gone Nick didn't try to grab a run; in any case, Blake had his hand raised like a traffic policeman to tell him not to attempt it.

There was no doubt in his mind that Jake would bang in another bouncer before the end of the over. He gambled it wouldn't be the next ball, since two bouncers in succession might draw a rebuke from the umpire. He was right again. The ball was on a good length, was straight and fast and Nick, on the back foot, cut. The ball practically whistled as it flew unstoppably to the boundary where it disappeared into undergrowth. This left the batsman in the princely position of being able to lean casually on his bat and grin at the bowler as various bodies scurried round to find the ball. He'd enjoyed making that stroke almost as much as he'd relished knocking back stumps in Winterton's innings. It was his day, all right. He couldn't remember the last time he'd felt as happy as this.

Not everybody was hunting for the ball. The crowd had been growing all afternoon, and now that school was over there were groups of pupils lounging about simply enjoying the sun and the cricket. Nick's fiery innings was drawing regular applause, and not only from his own team-mates.

The delay didn't improve Jake's temper. He was calculating when to throw in his next bouncer and it seemed to him he should do it now. Unfortunately for him, and Nick as it turned out, he got it all wrong. What he sent down was a full-toss; Nick went to meet it, missed, and it hit him sickeningly on the left foot, just at the point below the ankle where the training shoe he was wearing provided no protection at all. The pain was intense.

'Looks like a kangaroo that's just discovered itching powder!' was the cruellest of the jibes from spectators, many of whom simply were amused by the sight of an injured batsman hopping about in that manner.

'That'll teach him to hit our star bowler all over the place,' was another distinctly unsympathetic remark.

Even the umpire wasn't on the side of the victim. 'You know, it's downright silly to wear flimsy shoes like that; they'll never protect your feet,' he pointed out. 'Players should stick to proper cricket boots. Then you'd avoid this sort of trouble. Listen, if you want to go off the field to recover, you can. But if not, let's get on with the game without more delay.'

Nick didn't think the pain was easing much, but now he'd been given an ultimatum he had to carry on. He gave up massaging the tender spot and limped back to his crease. This time, Jake would probably try to get him on the other foot. Nick doubted that his opponent was good enough to bowl a true yorker.

Blake had hurried down the pitch to inquire about his well-being, motivated by concern for his own plight should Jake Sango bowl at him with his present aggression. 'I'll survive,' Nick told him through gritted teeth.

The fourth ball of what was to prove the most eventful over of an already memorable match was one of the best bouncers the Windmill had ever produced. Nick, still believing that his best response was to keep attacking, instinctively advanced down the wicket – and then had to duck swiftly to avoid being hit on the head. His arm had gone up in a defensive reflex and the ball struck him precisely on the point of the elbow.

The pain was excruciating, worse even than when his foot was hit. In his anguish and fury, Nick flung his bat to the ground and then clasped his elbow in his free hand. He didn't see that the ball had been promptly retrieved by the wicketkeeper who, removing the bails as calmly as could be, inquired: 'How's that?'

The umpire wasn't looking because this time he'd hurried down the pitch to see if bones were broken and whether the batsman needed professional medical attention. Jake was relishing his success, and being congratulated by two or three of his team-mates. The rest of the Winterton players had enough humanity in them to appear alarmed by the injury.

The pain was worse than anything Nick had ever experienced. He knew his eyes were full of tears, but he couldn't worry about what anybody might be thinking. The umpire was carefully examining his elbow to try to discover whether there was a fracture.

'It's the funny bone, you know,' he murmured consolingly. 'Awful name for it really; I know it's a terrible spot to be hit.'

Nick heard someone laughing about that, the wicketkeeper he guessed, but no one else was being quite so insensitive. His damaged foot was still painful, too, and all he could think of was getting back to the pavilion to lie down and try to recover. There was no way he could hold a bat again today.

'I'll help you off, if you like,' said Carl Waterfield, coming up with a faint smile in which sympathy blended with relief at getting an awkward opponent off the field and out of the match.

Cradling his arm, and with Carl kindly carrying his bat for him, Nick was just about to limp away when he heard the 'keeper repeat his earlier question: 'He is out, isn't he, umpire? I mean, he was *way* out of his crease when I removed the bails.'

And the umpire, looking just a trifle embarrassed, nodded. 'I have to say he was. Bad luck, really, but that's the risk in going down the pitch and playing a poor shot.'

Nick was in too much discomfort to protest against the injustice of the dismissal and the insult in the umpire's comment. He couldn't think straight about that or anything else.

Johnny Highton, coming to the boundary to meet him, asked how bad the pain was.

'*Very* bad, worst I've ever, ever had,' Nick gulped. Once again he felt fingers exploring the tenderest spot, but they neither reduced nor added to his pain. His foot was hardly less agonizing when he walked but it was pointless to complain about that.

'I'm pretty sure nothing's broken,' was Mr Highton's verdict. 'But you'd better go and sit down and see if it improves. And you can also reflect on your foolishness in flinging your bat down like that. Yes, I know you were hurt, and some reaction is understandable, but not in that manner. That's bad sportsmanship. The umpire would have been perfectly entitled to speak to you severely about showing dissent of that nature. I've told you all, every member of my teams, that displaying dissent at umpiring decisions won't be tolerated.'

'But, but I didn't even know I was out then,' Nick protested. 'Didn't know until I started to leave the wicket.'

'Look, do as I say, go and sit down and stay calm. That's the very best thing you can do, young Nicholas. We'll talk about the consequences of your actions later.'

The brightest of days had become the blackest of days for Nick. It wasn't just a return to the rain that had ushered in the day; a full-scale deluge from the darkest of clouds had come down, drowning his happiness, the happiness his wickets and runs had created. The pain from his injuries was only part of his depression – once again, his future as a member of the school's first XI was in doubt. It might not exist at all.

'You should immerse that in a bucket of ice,' observed Steven Lindley as Nick removed his trainer and sock and studied his clearly swelling foot. 'It'll bring the bruise out and stop the swelling.'

'Oh, and I'm just going to find that in one of the lockers, am I, the one packed full of chunks of Arctic iceberg?' Nick responded bitterly.

'Probably not,' Steven replied mildly, 'but if you go to the school I expect the caretaker could dig some out of a fridge in the kitchen. I'll fetch it for you if you like.'

'Thanks, Steve,' said Nick, grateful for such unexpected kindness, 'but I'll be able to manage. Do me good to get out of here.'

Stuffing the sock in his pocket, he forced his foot back into the shoe and hobbled away, using his bat as a form of crutch because the pain was no easier (though that in his elbow was thankfully receding). It was an effort to haul himself up the long flight of steps to the path that encircled the school. One or two people he encountered smiled sympathetically but no one offered to assist him, for which he was thankful. He didn't want to talk to anyone about anything.

It took some time to discover the whereabouts of the caretaker, various cleaners suggesting that he could be in one place and others saying somewhere else. Then, when he found him having a smoke outside the rear entrance to the gymnasium, the news was as grim as he might have predicted.

'Sorry, laddie, no chance of that,' the stick-thin, grey-haired caretaker grinned in response to Nick's request for the therapeutic ice. 'All the fridges are locked up when the kitchen staff leave. Full of valuable stuff, fridges, you know. Can't be too careful with fridges.'

Nick shrugged and turned away. The parting shot from the caretaker didn't surprise him. 'You look really hot and bothered; I can see why you need ice! Never mind, laddie, just sit down and have a rest and you'll cool down soon enough.'

A couple of minutes later Nick took that advice because he physically couldn't keep walking any longer without a rest. He lowered himself on to the grass bank beside the steps to the cricket field and tried to take an interest in the match. Adam Lexton was at the wicket and batting with obvious enthusiasm and a determination to go for his shots. Even Blake had come out of his shell and the Trimdon score was mounting briskly.

That was little comfort to Nick. He knew that he should still have been out there, hitting his highest score, leading the way to victory and securing his place in the team. Instead the roar of applause was for someone else.

In his frustration he seized his bat and smashed it down on the nearest step.

It broke in two.

Seven

As soon as he entered the kitchen, Nick sensed that his dad was in an argumentative mood. He had the morning paper propped up on the teapot and was shaking his head sorrowfully at some story he was reading, a sure sign he'd found something to disagree with or complain about. Even his grin, as he greeted his only son, could be interpreted as the prelude to some challenging remark.

'How's the wounded hero today, then?' he inquired, leaning back.

'I'm not wounded and I'm not a hero,' Nick retorted testily as he foraged in the fridge for eggs. 'The hero was Adam Lexton, so you should ask him.'

'Ah, a batsman, no doubt! Well, batsmen will always be heroes, they're what the public go to see, isn't that right? Great – '

'Actually, Adam's a bowler, like me,' Nick cut in, cracking eggs fiercely into a bowl before whipping them into a froth. 'He scored the runs that I would've got if I hadn't been unlucky. Luck, you know, does play a part in sport – even in your chummy little indoor bowls matches.'

'Hardly relevant, dear Nicholas, hardly relevant. Batsmen, I'm positive, make their own luck. Well, the great ones do, of course. You see, they're the aristo-crats of the game, bowlers the mere toilers in the paddy fields of sport. Ah, must remember that phrase! Come in useful again, no doubt.'

Nick continued to prepare his scrambled eggs, dropping butter and grated cheese into the pan and adding a pinch of salt. The pain in his foot had subsided into a dull ache with occasional twinges, but he was going to have to live with that; he must push himself through the pain barrier into complete fitness again. X-rays had showed there were no breaks in any of his bones so, really, he could play again as soon as he felt able to run in at top speed again. With Trimdon having defeated Winterton as a result of Adam's inspirational batting and Blake's sudden renewal of confidence Nick knew he couldn't afford to miss a match. His contribution to victory might quickly be forgotten if he lost his place in the side.

'Dad, I know you're just winding me up, but I'm not in the mood for it, OK?' he pointed out, while gently but firmly stirring the contents of the pan. 'To be honest, I was even thinking along those lines myself the other day. I mean, that batsmen *are* the lucky ones. They get to be captain, don't they, of most teams, especially international teams. Yet it's *bowlers* that win matches. Which is why I'm staying one, the best ever! Oh, and another thing, bowlers like me usually get a few runs as well, sometimes a lot. But batsmen, guys who can only bat, they never get wickets, do they? So they're of less use to a team.'

His dad laughed and gave in gracefully, but couldn't help adding: 'All right, I suppose you argued that pretty well, but don't forget that it's usually batsmen who get the knighthoods and make all the big money in sponsorship and so on. Bowlers just collect injuries, like you. Oh yes, and your big hero from Pakistan.'

Nick's fork, laden with toast and scrambled egg, was suspended half-way to his mouth as he digested news instead of food. 'Kamran Aslam, you mean?'

'The very same.'

'But what's happened to him? He's not really *injured*, is he?'

'According to this newspaper, he is. Got a severe blow to the knee from someone's full-blooded pull that your hero didn't manage to get a hand to. So he's not playing against Kent in the home match today. But he'll still be there to cheer his team-mates on, so the report says. Full of the right sort of team spirit, your hero, even if he is misguided enough to earn his living as a bowler.'

Nick grabbed the paper from his dad, open at the page of cricket reports.

'What rotten luck,' he pronounced when he'd devoured every detail of the account. 'I can really sympathize; I know just how he'll feel. You know, I think I ought to give him a ring and tell him that. He'd probably appreciate it. I know I would if he phoned me!'

'Well, why don't you?' his dad said, getting to his

feet. 'You members of the bowlers' union need to stick together against the rest of the world which is *always* against you! Anyway, it'll be my money paying for the call, won't it?'

'What phone call is that you're planning?' asked Nick's mum coming in to the kitchen. 'You haven't time to chat up your friends at this time of the day. I thought you and I were off to the beach in ten minutes, Nick. Before it gets crowded on a day like this. And you haven't even finished your breakfast yet!'

Hastily, Nick gulped more egg-and-toast. 'I'll be ready, Mum, don't worry about that. I'm not making a phone call now because he won't be there. But I should be able to get him as soon as we're back from the beach.'

'Who are we talking about, if I may ask?'

Silently he handed the paper to her, pointing to the appropriate report. 'Soon as I've finished this I'll brush my teeth and then we'll be off. Leave the washing-up. I'll do it when we get back. Promise!'

She raised her eyebrows as she scanned the report but made no comment. Chores in the Freeland household were spread fairly and one of the good things about Nick, she told everyone, was that he never complained about doing his share. 'But surely you'd have liked a daughter?' people sometimes remarked. 'You can share so much when a girl's growing up.' Mrs Freeland said she supposed that was true, but she was perfectly content with all that she shared with her only son.

'We're not going to do *only* stamina-building exercises are we, Mum?' he inquired anxiously as he slid into the front passenger seat of her red BMW. He hoped to own a similar car himself one day.

'I should hope I can be a bit more inventive than that,' she grinned. 'I don't want you to risk your foot unnecessarily before it's had a proper chance to heal.'

She parked beside the futuristic-looking new leisure centre but they headed straight for the rolling dunes. Nick glanced enviously at the swimsuited people of his own age frolicking in the gentle waves rolling on to the beach, but he knew his mother wouldn't allow any time off for swimming until the training session was over.

From a kangaroo-pouch-like bag strapped round her waist she produced a couple of cricket balls and explained: 'Look, I think this'll be a useful exercise, not just for improving the suppleness of your muscles but to give you some catching practice. While we're running I'll keep turning or backing away and then I'll chuck a ball at you. You have to catch it, of course! And I'll throw a second almost immediately, so you've got to grab that with the other hand, OK? You'll probably be off balance sometimes, but that's what this is all about, adapting to circumstances, just as you do on the field. All the time, we keep on the move, up one dune, down the next. But if your foot starts to give you pain, Nick – real pain, not just a titchy ache – then tell me at once and we'll stop. Got that?'

He nodded and then, grinning, said, 'I've got just

one question: what happens when I've got both hands full?'

'You keep your temper and you lob them back to me. Lob, mind; don't hurl them as if I were a wicket-keeper. Right, let's go.'

Nick was soon thankful that, like his mother, he was wearing no more than shorts and a T-shirt as he toiled up and down the sandy slopes in the strengthening sun. More than once he slithered sideways after stretching for a ball going away from him and twice he actually pancaked down one descent. Yet, for her part, Sallie Freeland looked as cool as ever as she collected the lobbed returns and threw the balls back from a variety of angles. Much of the time she was moving backwards but that didn't seem to trouble her in any way at all. Until, suddenly, she *did* lose her footing and slid all the way down a gentle slope on her bottom.

He didn't laugh, because it wasn't really funny, and anyway, he was panting too much. But it did give him a chance of a breather.

'So, you're human after all!' he smiled as he held out his hand to haul her back up the dune. 'Thought you never made a mistake!'

'Don't kid yourself about that, I just try to keep my mistakes to myself,' she said, reaching into the capacious pouch to produce a couple of cans of fruit juice. 'Here,' she said, tossing one to him, 'you deserve a break – and so do I. Must say, the day seems to be hotting up by the minute. We won't overdo it. Training should be enjoyable, not an ordeal.'

If he'd heard that phrase from her once, he'd heard it a thousand times. He said 'Cheers!' as he raised the can to his lips and drank deeply. Already he was thinking about what he'd say to Kamran if he managed to get hold of him on the telephone. What bothered him was the thought that the Pakistan paceman might not be willing to take a call from a complete stranger. Although they'd met, Nick hadn't given him his name.

'Come on, stop day-dreaming about your next five-wicket haul!' she told him sharply, tidily replacing the empty cans in the pouch. 'Must say, your left-handed catching is improved. Perhaps one of these days we can practise your left-handed throwing. Nothing like being ambidextrous to take the opposition by surprise.'

'Caught a beauty in the nets recently,' Nick told her. 'Even old Highbrow would have praised it if he hadn't been in such a foul mood at the time. Everybody else thought it was great.'

For the next couple of minutes they kept up the new routine until, darting through a narrow gap between two high dunes, they almost bumped into a boy who, instinctively, reached up and caught the ball intended for Nick. Recognition was instantaneous.

'Well, well, so this is where you do your secret training, is it?' smirked Red Allan, Rochbury's opening bowler. 'Not surprised you have to keep it a secret if you need to get a girlfriend to play cricket with you. You'll never get to play with the big boys that way!'

'But – but – ' Nick stammered, not knowing how to reply. He could feel a redness in his face that had nothing to do with his physical exertions.

Red, however, wasn't stopping to hear any explanations. Tossing the ball high into the air so that Nick would have to move to catch it, he turned to the pal he was with and, putting his arm round his shoulder, moved away.

'Stupid idiot!' Nick muttered, his embarrassment still evident.

'Who's he?' Mrs Freeland inquired, looking in the direction the pair had gone, her eyebrows still arched. 'He may be idiotic to you but I must say he was quite flattering to me. But then he didn't take time to look too closely, did he?'

'Vigor Allan, though he likes to be called Red. Opens the bowling for Rochbury, one of the schools we play. Seems to think he's the best fast bowler around. But he hasn't seen the best of me yet.'

Nick didn't know what to say about the 'girlfriend' remark. It wasn't the first time his mother had been mistaken for someone younger. Because she was only nineteen when Nick was born, and she still was slim and retained her youthful looks, one or two people had guessed that she was his sister. Nick himself wasn't sure how he felt about having a mother who all too obviously was different from most of the mums he encountered with his school mates.

She didn't ask any further questions about Red, but a few minutes later, after she'd noticed him wince, she said, 'Right, I think we'll give up for today. Good work-out, I reckon. How's your foot now?'

'Not too bad. Just a bit sore, I suppose. But the doc said it would take time for the bruise to come out, so I expected that.'

'Better just try bowling one over when we can find a flat stretch,' she said, changing her mind. 'I want to watch your action off the shorter run. Can you do that?'

'Sure,' he responded, and demonstrated that he had lost none of his rhythm or pace when they found the firm strip that was needed.

Sallie, standing to one side to observe everything critically, nodded her approval. 'Very good, really good. I think this boy Charlie has done me out of a job. Mind you, I did try to get you to cut down your run before, didn't I? But sometimes you're so stubborn! Still, I hope this has finally convinced you that length of run-up bears little relation to final pace generated. Agreed?'

'If you say so, Mum,' he smiled.

As soon as they were home again he looked up the telephone number for the County Ground and punched it out. While he waited for the ring to be answered he wondered idly whether he would know it by heart before long because it would be his own work number. To his surprise, he was told that Kamran was in the dressing-room and they could put him through right away. Nick moistened his lips and hastily rehearsed his opening sentence.

98

'Yes, who is this?' was the distinctive answering voice.

'Oh, hi. I don't suppose you'll remember me but I gave you some of my ice-cream when you were fielding during Ben Hardman's benefit match. Well – '

'Sure I do. Never happened to me before. Sorry, but I can't give it back to you!'

'No, no, that's all right,' Nick said hurriedly, not able to cope with a joke just yet. 'I, er, well, I just wanted to say I'm sorry to hear you've damaged your knee. I just want to wish you luck, that it gets better soon.'

'Well, man, that's really great of you, most thoughtful. But tell me, please, what's your name? I don't know it, do I?'

'No, no, I never mentioned it at Hopton Park. My name's Nick Freeland. I'm a bowler, too, for my school team. Actually, I'm sort of injured as well. Got hit on the foot while batting.'

There was the briefest pause and then Kamran Aslam said enthusiastically, 'I remember now, you said you wished you could bowl like me. I've just been thinking; maybe we should see if you can.'

'Can what?' Nick couldn't really think what he meant. Just the fact that he was talking directly to his hero was beginning to unnerve him.

'Can bowl like me!' was the jovial reply. 'Just hang on a little moment, Nick, please.'

Nick could hear some half-whispered conversation going on in the background as well as a sudden burst of applause and cheering. The county, he guessed, must be doing well and the home dressing-room was celebrating. In the brief interval before Kamran spoke again Nick tried to work out what was in Kamran's mind. Was he beginning to imagine that it was a hoax call, some sort of joke being tried out for a bet? Or –

'Yes, all can be well if you can come to the county nets a week on Sunday in the morning,' was the astonishing announcement in Nick's ear. 'Do you think you can do that?'

'Well, yes, I'm sure I can,' Nick managed to agree. 'But what – '

'We're holding a trial for promising players,' the bowler went on serenely. 'It is before our afternoon match and it starts at 10.30. I have just checked that time. Rob Hastie – you know, our county coach – well, he'll be in charge. But I hope to be there, too. No, I *will* be there. So, we can meet again, Nick.'

'But that, that's *wonderful*. I really can't believe it. Kamran, that's marvellous news. I don't know how to thank you.'

'You don't have to do that, just come along and show that you can be a top-class bowler in the making. The county always needs stars for tomorrow. Oh, you will be fit by then, won't you? Your injury is not serious?'

'No, no, it's almost better now,' Nick assured him. 'And, well, I hope *you* are fit, too. I can't wait to meet you properly.'

'I will look forward to that, Nick. Thank you for

telephoning me. I must go now, so, good-bye for the moment.'

The line went dead but Nick was in such a state of suppressed excitement it was a few seconds before he remembered to replace the receiver. A trial at the county nets – and watched by the fastest bowler in the world, Kamran Aslam! Wow! And then Nick had another thought and promptly amended that description: the *current* fastest bowler in the world.

Eight

Nick peered up at the sky through the windscreen and shook his head despairingly. 'Why am I so unlucky?' he wanted to know. 'Why does it *always* have to rain on my special days, the days that can change my life?'

His mother flicked through the gears to overtake a wandering cyclist and then a milk float. 'Nonsense! You really do exaggerate. I told you it would start off as a grey day and then clear up. That's what'll happen. Anyway, even if it doesn't improve they have the indoor school, so that can be used instead.'

Nick's face brightened instantly. 'Hey, d'you know, I'd forgotten that.' Then he started to frown again. 'But that wouldn't be the same. They've got to see what I can do on grass. That's the important thing.'

'*Nicholas*! Stop it!' she ordered fiercely. 'You'll get out there, you'll bowl and this cloud cover will help the ball to swing. Well, that's the universal theory, though I've never seen it proved by anyone or anything. Something to do with a change of air pressure, so they say. Anyway your luck's *in*, not out. Remember that. Oh, and remember this, too: don't try to bowl *too* fast. Pace is not everything, not with people as experienced as Rob Hastie. He'll be much more impressed by control, line and length. Speed comes later. So, just take things calmly, OK?'

'If you say so, Mum,' he smiled. 'You know I *always* listen to my favourite coach.'

'I don't believe that for a moment,' she replied. 'You certainly didn't listen to me when I originally told you about your run-up. You listened to somebody else about that. Still, as long as you *do* learn, that's what really matters.'

When, a few minutes later, she dropped him at the entrance gates to the County Ground and wished him luck he managed to remember to say: 'Oh, and good luck with your match, too. Hope you're in brilliant form – like me!'

Before passing through the impressive, wrought-iron gates into the famous arena he glanced about in the hope of catching sight of Denis Demarco. His best friend had promised to 'drop in to see you mixing with the high and mighty', but for undisclosed reasons preferred to make his own way to the ground. Nick suspected that was because he didn't fancy getting up so early on a Sunday morning!

As nonchalantly as he could manage, he made his way round behind the main grandstand to the nets set up on the far side of the ground. There was hardly anyone about and for a few moments he had the horrible suspicion that he'd come on the wrong day. But that was ridiculous! The county were playing Somerset that afternoon and he remembered precisely what Kamran had told him. Then, to his distinct relief, two boys of about his own age suddenly emerged from a doorway below the players' balcony.

'Hi, have you been invited for coaching as well?' the taller of the pair greeted him in a welcoming manner. When Nick nodded he went on, 'We can use the room in there for our kit if we want to. They said they'll put out some soft drinks for us – oh, and there's a loo for those who are overcome with nerves!'

'Well, I'm fine at the moment,' Nick responded, and they all laughed. They exchanged names and Nick found he was with Luke, who was from Wheathouse College, and Jamie, who attended Jordanston School. Both said they batted a bit but really regarded themselves as bowlers. They weren't giving much away and Nick couldn't tell whether that was natural caution or modesty. He declared himself to be a pace bowler and they just nodded without asking for other details.

Then he spotted the stocky, blond-haired figure of Rob Hastie, the county coach, strolling towards the nets in the company of a couple of second XI players. One of them was James Tanfield, a batsman Nick had actually played against with Arkenley. They all appeared to be in a relaxed mood and it occurred to Nick that there was an air of casualness about the entire scene. It wasn't easy to believe that, on a morning like this, an ambitious young cricketer might achieve something that would so impress the experts that his life would be changed for ever. And yet, he knew, there wasn't much point in turning up for such an occasion if you didn't want to reach the heights as a player. Nick was sure he'd prove to be as good a player as any of those present. So why, he couldn't help wondering, hadn't he been invited to this session *officially*? If he hadn't taken the initiative to ring Kamran on another matter altogether then he'd have missed out completely. To say the least, that would have been unfortunate – for the club just as much as for himself, he believed.

As if alerted by some hidden and silent signal, other youngsters also arrived from various directions. Shortly, Rob Hastie, tossing a cricket ball from one hand to the other as if to show that action would soon take place, waved everyone into a circle around him.

'Good to see you, fellas, so thanks for accepting our invitation this morning,' the coach, who was also captain of the county's second XI, greeted them. 'As you were told, it's your bowling we're interested in. We want to get an idea of the talent we've got on our doorstep. We're always looking to the future, you know, and some of you guys may very well *be* our future stars.'

He paused for that to sink in. Although glances were exchanged among his audience, no one dared to say a word.

'So, we're going to give you a chance to bowl your best against two of the stars just ahead of you in the queue for top billing, James Tanfield and Tom Ashcroft.' He pointed them out, somewhat unneces-sarily, and smiled expansively. 'Well, they won't want their stumps shattered by anyone so they'll *murder* your bowling if you let 'em, won't you?'

Dutifully, his team-mates nodded, though they looked a trifle embarrassed.

'But first we need to warm up a bit, relax the muscles, make sure we don't snap anything, so we'll do a bit of running and catching. As you see, the catching cradle has been rolled out. My batting stars and I will throw a few balls in there and you young 'uns can run around and catch 'em, if you can. Right, let's get going.'

When fired fiercely into the shallow oval of the cradle, balls shot out again off the smooth wooden surface at unpredictable angles and so anyone chasing round the circuit had to be prepared for anything. It was a lively, often amusing and always exciting experience as players competed for chances to make a safe or sometimes spectacular catch, cheered on by the trio hurling the balls into the mini-crater.

'God, that's really warmed me up!' gasped Luke to Nick as at last the coach called a halt to the task. 'And I thought it was going to be cool today. The weather, I mean!'

Nick looked round to see whether Denis had surfaced yet, but there was still no sign of him; perhaps he'd decided to give it a miss. However, coming into view was someone he recognized instantly: Red Allan. It seemed a bit of a coincidence that the Rochbury bowler should turn up at the same place as himself only a week after they'd last met. Surely he couldn't be following him? No, impossible!

It must be that Allan, too, had received an invitation as a promising bowler. Nick turned away. He didn't want to be on the end of any more stupid jibes.

'Come on, then. Yes, you with the long black hair,' Rob Hastie was saying and, guiltily, Nick realized who he meant. Plainly, the coach was compiling some sort of list on the clipboard he was holding.

'Sorry,' said Nick, going up to him.

'It's all right but I've got to get everybody's name down and it's easier to do that now before we start letting people bowl. Right, who are you, where are you from and what do you bowl?'

Nick supplied the details and was told he'd be second in line to bowl in the first net against Tom Ashcroft, who was now fussily preparing himself to bat, double-checking pads and gloves and adjusting the visor of his helmet. It hadn't occurred to Nick that the county batsmen would wear maximum protection against the bowling of a group of, it had to be admitted, mere schoolboys. On the other hand, perhaps he was just making sure no one would injure him if they slipped in a beamer or a rocketing bouncer. And it was that thought that triggered off a slight attack of nerves on his own part, for he couldn't forget the beamer he'd let slip in the Rochbury match.

'Right, let's see what you can do,' the coach said a few minutes later, tossing him a ball that was, to say the least, rather worn. Nick had imagined he might even be provided with a new ball but, now he thought about it, he supposed it was obvious the club wouldn't go to that expense just for a trial for juniors.

His run-up was all it should have been, but just before he reached his delivery stride he realized he was going to over-step the makeshift crease. Trying to adjust much too late, he sent down a ball that would have been a wide in any form of cricket. Tom simply blinked, looking pained as the ball barely bounced and finished up in the side-netting.

'Sorry,' Nick apologized generally as he heard sniggers from some of those waiting their turn to perform.

'Don't worry about it, everybody's entitled to a loosener before getting into the swing of things,' Rob remarked genially, employing a favourite phrase for such circumstances. 'Just make sure you get the next one right, son.'

'That's what happens when you play cricket with *girls*!' someone said loudly, and Nick knew without turning round that it was Red Allan.

'What did you say?' Rob asked immediately in the sort of tone that demanded a proper reply.

Red, however, wasn't fazed by that. 'Saw him myself the other day, having catching practice with a girl. It was in the sand dunes actually and – '

'That was my mother, not a girlfriend,' Nick retorted. Although he wasn't shouting it was loud enough for everyone to hear.

That admission, astonishing to most listeners, was received in stunned silence, apart from one half-strangled laugh.

Rob, glancing at his clipboard again, suddenly turned back to Nick. 'Nick *Freeland*. So, would your mother be Sallie Freeland, by any chance? The England women's team all-rounder?'

'That's right, she's my coach. She brought me up to play cricket right from the start, just as soon as I was big enough to hold a ball and throw it properly.'

'Well, well, well! No wonder you've got such a good action,' Rob said thoughtfully. 'Very talented bowler, your mum. Good enough for most men's teams in my view. And she can bat a bit, too, can't she? Well, she could the last time I saw her playing for a mixed team – must have been Scarborough last season, Festival time.'

Nick knew by now that everyone was looking at him but no one was saying a word. It was the first time his mother's cricketing background had ever been discussed in front of strangers who were all involved in the game. From experience, and from what she had related to him herself, he knew that not everyone had a high regard for women's cricket, even at inter-national level. Other people who had seen her play had made the same sort of remark about her being 'good enough' for men's cricket, but it was never what she wanted to hear. After all, the Women's World Cup Final at Lord's in the early 1990s had shown television audiences what skills and determination they possessed.

'Well, young Nick, I'm glad you've come to join us,' Rob went on genially. 'Give your mum my regards when you get home. Oh yes, and don't let her down by bowling another ball as bad as the last one!'

Because the coach smiled broadly to take any sting out of the last remark, everyone else relaxed again. Nick suddenly felt grateful to Red Allan for making his original comment. It couldn't be doubted, from the expressions on their faces, that most of the boys were thoroughly impressed by Rob Hastie's reaction to the disclosure that Nick's mother was an international cricketer. It had definitely raised his standing with all of them, even with Red, who was looking discomfited. All the same, Nick didn't want to be regarded simply as the son of a talented cricketer. He was determined to be known as a future England player himself.

When the action resumed and it came to Nick's turn again, he collected a ball that was in altogether better condition. Everyone, he guessed, would be watching him this time, apart from the batsman and bowler using the second net. Taking his time over beginning his run, he gathered pace with every stride, felt he'd hit the spot perfectly and sent the ball whistling down the narrow channel. Tom Ashcroft, who'd hit the previous ball for what looked like half a mile back past the bowler, was pushed back on to his stumps but still wasn't able to save himself. The ball on a full length beat the forward prod and knocked the leg stump over.

Applause rang out, genuine appreciation of a very fine delivery. 'Well done! Just the ticket, Nick,' Rob Hastie carolled.

Delighted though he was with his success, Nick couldn't help wondering why it was that his first ball on vital occasions was either brilliant or rubbish. He would have to learn to be consistent, that was plain. But he was thrilled that this time the batsman himself signalled that he'd been beaten by 'a good 'un'. Nick nodded his thanks.

'Well, what are you thinking I could teach you after bowling a ball like that?' he heard a voice say. Instantly he knew who it was.

'Kamran! Hey, I didn't see you! But –' Nick stopped, fearful of saying too much.

'Well, I saw you, Nick. Great ball.'

Now the rest of the trial bowlers were looking even more bewildered. Did everyone who was anybody know Nick Freeland? It seemed so. Even the county's star overseas player was on first name terms with the tall, dark-haired Trimdon boy.

'No wonder he's got blue eyes,' Red Allan murmured about his rival to no one in particular; but those who heard felt he'd simply expressed their own thoughts.

'Well, you should have seen the previous ball,' Nick grinned. 'Total disaster!'

'Don't worry your head about the bad ones when you can produce one as good as that,' Kamran advised. 'We all send down garbage balls from time to time. Makes the batsman believe we can't be that good after all. Then we get him out next ball with the unplayable one! That's how the magic works, eh, Nick?'

'Er, yes,' replied Nick weakly, feeling he had to say something.

It struck him as simply amazing that his bowling hero was not only talking to him in this familiar way, but even expressing Nick's own thoughts about bowling (except that he himself hadn't yet learned to ignore his bad experiences).

'Glad you could turn up,' Kamran went on in his friendly manner. 'How's your bad foot?'

Momentarily, Nick couldn't think what he was talking about because he'd got over that problem days ago. 'Oh, fine now, thanks. Actually, I'm a quick healer – like my mum. Lucky for me. What about your knee?'

Kamran laughed. 'We sound like a couple of old men, don't we, concerned only about our health! Well, it's no problem now, just another old bruise to fade away. You get used to that in this game, don't you? Let's talk about your bowling. Your action looks good. You have obviously been well coached. Your run-up is smooth. You generate good pace. Do you get the ball to swing regularly?'

'Sometimes, but not as often as I'd like. It's often a matter of luck, isn't it? You know, the state of the pitch and the weather, cloud cover and so on. But – '

He stopped because Kamran was shaking his head vigorously. 'Not just luck, oh no. You the bowler, you have to *make* things work in your favour. The grip, that is very important. How you hold the ball, that makes all the difference to your success.'

Nick hadn't expected to receive what amounted to private tuition from his hero, but he sensed now that he could learn something that could add an extra dimension to his prowess as a bowler. One or two of the other trialists moved cautiously towards them as if keen to hear something that might be useful to them, too. One had produced a slip of paper and a pen from his pocket and Nick hoped the boy wouldn't be so stupid as to ask for an autograph *now*.

Kamran called to Rob for a ball and nonchalantly caught the one thrown to him. 'Look,' he told Nick and the rest of his audience, 'you must try – try very, very hard – to keep the wrist behind the ball for as long as possible when you are about to bowl. That will keep the seam pointing in the right direction and gives the ball a chance to swing.'

He paused, flexing his wrist and then changing his hold on the ball by a fraction. 'You should find that, instead of just straightening off the seam now and then, it will move as you want it to. Well, it will if you get everything right!'

They all dutifully smiled and those who bowled fast inwardly vowed to try that out at the earliest opportunity. Only Nick, however, was given the chance to test the Kamran theory immediately.

'Go on, Nick, it's your turn again, I think,' the Pakistani urged. 'It may take a very long time to get your grip right, so you must start right away.'

Although it felt awkward as he ran in, his rhythm was unaffected and his aim as good as it had been with the previous ball. Once again Tom Ashcroft played and missed, but this time the ball swung away so late he was very fortunate indeed not to get a thin edge that could have provided a catch to first slip.

'Good ball, *very* good,' Kamran applauded. 'I must take up proper coaching in future if I can get all my pupils to do things right the first time I ask them!'

'Don't suppose it will always happen like that,' Nick remarked, tempering his own joy at such success with a vision of reality.

'No, indeed,' Kamran agreed. 'But perseverance will bring rewards. That is the fate of the fast bowler, you know: to mix perseverance with perspiration!'

Nick and two of the other players, both of whom bowled fast, instinctively and jokingly wiped imaginary sweat from their foreheads and they and the rest laughed. Rob, delighted to find the group so relaxed, came over to chat to them and Kamran. Soon there was a change round in the bowling and batting arrangements and Kamran himself strapped on pads for a net.

'Just what I need,' he announced. 'Felt a bit out of touch lately and the skipper says I've got to contribute some runs as well as wickets.'

Hard though they tried, nobody managed to capture the prize of his wicket. As he'd already scored 86 in one Test-match innings that was hardly surprising, but Nick still believed he could beat him for swing and pace. The wrist-behind-ball technique wasn't as easy to manage as he'd first thought and he struggled now and again to get the delivery right. In the manner of the true professional, Kamran treated every ball he received from everyone on its merits and therefore he hammered Nick's weak deliveries.

As he waited to take his turn to bowl at Kamran or, in the other net, Rob Hastie, he wished the county coach would suggest he might like to have a bat, too. It would be wonderful to have the chance to face Kamran Aslam's tornado-like in-swingers. Probably he wouldn't be good enough to get a bat on any of them, but he might be lucky. Above all, it would be illuminating to see, from a batsman's position, how fast the ball came to him. Of course, it was highly likely the pace would be so great the ball would simply blast the bat out of his hands. Still, even that would be something to boast about! 'I faced the world's fastest bowler. He bowled with such speed he actually knocked the bat out of my hands. But I survived. He didn't get me out!'

Unfortunately, it didn't happen. Such an idea either didn't occur to Rob or there was no time for it. In any case, Nick reflected, perhaps Kamran really did need to practise his batting at a time he wasn't ready to risk his knee with unnecessary bowling.

'OK, boys, that's it,' Rob announced after a quick glance at his watch. 'Thank you all for coming. Hope you enjoyed yourselves and found out useful things about your own bowling skills. We have all your names and details so we can get in touch when we've got space for you again. Right, see you.'

Nick experienced a sense of disappointment. It was all over! His meeting with his hero, his opportunity to bowl in the nets at the County Ground against semi-professional batsmen, his triumph in bowling one of them out with a brilliant delivery, the personal tuition from the best pace bowler in the world – all finished. Something that meant everything to him seemingly meant nothing, or hardly anything, to the club. Was it a classic case of 'Don't call us, we'll call you?'

'Oh, yeah, Nick and Luke – could you just hang on a moment, please?' he heard Rob Hastie sing out.

They turned as one, hope suddenly returning. Were they going to be treated as special cases after all?

Rob, with Kamran at his shoulder, came to meet them. 'You did excellently today, excellently,' he declared with evident enthusiasm. 'If you can build on those standards you'll have a future in the game. So, we'd like to see more of you, see how you progress when up against serious opposition in match conditions. I don't need to tell you that cricket is a game of character as well as skill. How a player conducts himself in the cauldron of a fiercely competitive game is as important as whether he can bowl line and length. You know that?'

The boys nodded in unison, still uncertain what might be coming next. But he'd singled them out from the other trialists and therefore they'd found favour with the coach to one of England's top county teams. Nick's mouth was suddenly dry and there was a tingle of excitement running through his whole body.

'So I'm going to send you official invitations to turn out for one of our club sides on a regular basis. The matches'll be at weekends, of course, so we hope you'll be free to play for us,' the coach said. 'If you make the progress we expect, the sky's the limit. You could be tomorrow's county players. So, boys, what d'you feel about that?'

'Great!' exclaimed Nick. 'Brilliant!' responded Luke.

'Are you two mates – play for the same school team?' Rob went on.

Luke laughed. 'Hardly! We're actually rivals, I suppose. Nick goes to Trimdon and I'm at Wheat-house College. We play each other in a Schools Cup match in a fortnight. So – '

Nick had been thinking about the possibility of one day playing in the same team as Kamran and the question Luke answered so surprisingly had almost by-passed him. He'd come to regard Red Allan as a rival but now it seemed that Luke might be one instead!

'Well, if you boys are on opposite sides I think I should be there,' Kamran suddenly announced, much to Nick's surprise. 'So, Luke, can you give me details of when and where the match takes place?'

While Luke did so Nick wondered whether he would get the chance to talk to Kamran on his own and learn some more of his bowling skills. Luke, of course, might have exactly the same ambitions.

'Good,' said Kamran, having heard all he needed. He turned to Nick. 'And if I can be there I shall buy you an ice-cream, even if it is a cold day! I think I owe you one!'

'Great, Kamran, thanks very much,' replied Nick, relieved by that personal touch. 'Just hope I get a few wickets to prove I've listened to your advice.'

And when he said that he deliberately avoided catching Luke's eye.

Nine

'Listen,' said Nick's mother, 'I'll do my level best to get to the ground as soon as possible. With these marketing meetings you never know how long they'll go on. Depends on the client and how many nuts and bolts they want to tighten! But, Nick, I'll be there, I promise. I'll keep my fingers crossed that Trimdon bat first so I can definitely be there to see you bowl.'

'OK,' he said, preparing to get out of the car which she'd managed to slot into a space on a double yellow line just beyond the school entrance.

'So, have a good day and don't think *only* about cricket. All right?'

'Sure,' he said, closing the car door behind him. Both the sliding roof and the windows were open to make the most of the day. 'Hope your meeting goes well, Mum. See you.'

It wasn't easy to follow her advice to concentrate on other things such as maths and humanities, although drama was all right because he could transform himself into someone else for a play reading. All the time he had to keep an eye on the weather in case blue skies and scudding clouds and a bright sun gave way to rain (he wasn't as convinced as his mother about the reliability of meteorological forecasts). In fact, the wind *was* becoming more blustery and he guessed it could affect his bowling if it blew diagonally across the pitch at Wheathouse. But, as he'd never played there before, he really didn't know what to expect. Charlie Yorke, fast recovering from his injury but still unable to play again, said it was 'a reasonable sort of place with a pitch that's usually pretty true'. In other words, bowlers couldn't expect any real help from the pitch itself; wickets would have to be worked for all the time.

It was with Charlie that he'd discussed Johnny Highton's reaction to his account of his call-up to the county nets and the help he'd received from Kamran Aslam. Mr Highton hadn't seemed impressed in the slightest, to Nick's disappointment. 'In fact, I got the idea that he didn't think it was even worth *mentioning*. He didn't ask about future plans – you know, whether the county wanted me again for more training. Don't you think that's a bit weird, Charlie?'

Charlie shook his head dismissively. 'No, that's just him. Jealousy, you see. Plain, downright jealousy. He treats me in the same way, really.'

Nick stared in disbelief. 'I don't get it.'

'Simple. Johnny Highton didn't get to the top himself as a fast bowler and that's what he desperately wanted to do. Play for the county, England, usual stuff. But he never got beyond youth level in a representative game. He always says selectors can't recognise gold when they see it, when it gleams right in front of their eyes. That's why he never puts any names forward to the county for consideration, reckons that's a waste of time. He has a theory that they only pick boys from the private sector, anyway, so he's got a grievance about that, too. But he still loves the game, anybody can see that. In one way I can sort of sympathize with him because I know he feels that he doesn't want any young player today to be disappointed the way he was.'

'How d'you know all this?' Nick, fascinated, wanted to know.

'A mate of my dad's used to play in the same club side as old Highbrow and he used to hear him in the dressing-room moaning on about the shortcomings of idiotic selectors. He'd just started teaching then and apparently used to swear he'd never let any boy he taught suffer the same fate from selectors who couldn't see further than the end of their pug noses!'

Nick smiled at that description. But it did help to explain why the maths master and cricket coach displayed so little regard for either the promise or the successes of the pace bowlers who turned out for Trimdon School. It also meant, though, that if praise wasn't forthcoming from him that didn't mean it hadn't been earned. Therefore, it was just as well that Nick had managed to attract the interest of the county through his own efforts in front of their chief assessor, Rob Hastie. Perhaps, he reflected, Charlie Yorke, too, was a little jealous of Nick's success in that direction. But, if so, he didn't show it. Charlie remained cheerful and friendly and didn't seem dismayed at not being able to play against Wheathouse College.

Lawrie Bellamey, on the other hand, was practically ecstatic at the prospect of returning to the side after missing the previous match because of a violin exam. Because of what Mr Highton described as his 'stickability', Blake Carberry had been moved up to open the batting with Timbo Thomson and thus Lawrie could be slotted in at No. 5. Nick was pleased to learn that he'd bat at No. 7 – 'if we lose enough wickets to get down to you', as Craig Gooding remarked. He wasn't sure whether that was intended to be a compliment or not. Probably the skipper was just quoting the coach, Nick decided eventually.

It wasn't Craig's style to try to whip up any kind of fervour for their performance when he had a word with everyone in the dressing-room as they gathered before the match. Yet there couldn't be any doubt in anyone's mind that this was a game Trimdon wanted to win. There was a trophy at stake and Ross the Boss had even referred to it during the school assembly that morning, commenting that he was sure everyone would be 'wishing the school's cricket team success this afternoon in their quest to collect some silverware for us to display in the cabinet in the entrance hall'. The Headmaster added that he hoped to be present 'to witness our triumph. So, good luck to Mr Highton and his boys.'

He wasn't there, however, when the captains went out to toss up, but plenty of other spectators were scattered round the ground which stood on a plateau with two football pitches at a lower level beyond a line of poplars. Nets had been set up behind an old-style, mainly wooden pavilion, and Nick took the earliest opportunity to work up a good pace, although, naturally, he was still hoping that Trimdon would bat first. These days, he reflected, he seemed to spend almost too much time bowling into a netted corridor while aching to perform on a real wicket. Then again, that was probably part of the daily routine during the season for county players forever trekking from one ground to another around the country.

'They've won the toss and put us in!' Adam Lexton reported jubilantly to Nick and Lawrie after watching what was going on. 'You'd better swing the bat instead of the ball, Nick. I'll send a few down if you like.'

'What's he like, then, this opening bowler of theirs, the one you met at the county nets?' Lawrie wanted to know as they made their way towards the pavilion for the start of the match.

'Er, sharpish, I expect,' was all Nick could say. 'I mean, he looked OK when I saw him, but I wasn't exactly spending the time viewing the opposition.'

'No, just getting private bowling lessons from Kamran Aslam, that's all!' exclaimed Adam. 'Honestly, some guys grab all the luck going. *I'm* the one who needs help in that department. You're sharpish enough already, Freeland. But I'm warning you, I'm going to get more wickets today. My star sign says I could pick up a pot of gold at the end of the rainbow this afternoon!'

Nick pointed to the sky. 'No rain clouds about, so not much chance of a rainbow over Wheathouse, Ads.'

He also took a long glance around the arena in the hope of spotting a familiar face, even though he was sure he'd have known already if Kamran had turned up. The promise to attend the match hadn't been followed up by any other contact between them so Nick had no way of knowing whether the Pakistan pace bowler even knew his way to the college or what time the match was due to start. He did wonder whether Kamran had been in touch with Luke, but he wasn't keen to ask Luke that in case the answer was yes. Luke had struck him as friendly at all times, but so far today all they'd managed was a nod of recognition before the Wheathouse boy had to hurry away to a pre-match talk by the college coach.

Before he left home, Nick had made the firmest of vows to himself: 'Doesn't matter how many wickets Luke Penhale gets, I am going to get more!'

'Come on, let's go and sit there beside the sightscreen,' Adam suggested. 'Then we can see if the ball moves much – oh, and enjoy the slaughter as well. Timbo's dying to get 50 today. Says he's due a big innings.'

Nick nodded and Lawrie, eavesdropping, said he'd like to join them. With eyes sparkling and ready to chat away with anyone about anything, Lawrie looked to Nick as if he were still too young to have arrived at secondary school. His pre-batting nerves, however, invariably gave way to iron resolution and confident stroke-play when he got to the wicket.

Luke's opening delivery was, typically, a loosener and Timbo despatched it summarily through the covers for a boundary. Nick sympathized with Luke's scowl of self-reproach – no bowler wants to serve up such easy fare at any stage of a match, but allowing the batter to hammer your first ball for four presents the opposition with the idea that you can't be much good.

There wasn't much wrong with the rest of the over, however, and Timbo sensibly played each ball on its merits, which meant he didn't add to his score. The ball didn't deviate at all from a benign pitch but Luke was working up a brisk pace and had slotted into an attacking line and length. None of that was matched by his fellow opening bowler and yet it was in his over that Trimdon's first wicket fell.

Blake Carberry, keen to get off the mark, drove the fourth ball he received back past the bowler and yelled for a couple. Haring to the other end, head down, he didn't see that the fielder at long on had moved in like a sprinter from the blocks. Blake, spinning round for the second run, barely hesitated when Timbo gave an alarmed cry: 'No, no, wait!' Blake kept going and that relentlessness provoked Timbo into running too. Then, looking behind him at last, Blake saw the danger – skidded to a halt – and turned back.

The fielder sensibly chose to hurl the ball to his 'keeper – and the 'keeper had the simplest task of gently removing the bails to leave Timbo stranded, run out.

'Oh no, the stupid jerk!' Adam exploded. 'What a crazy way to lose a wicket. The second run was never on there.'

Everybody else seemed to know that except Blake, who tried to apologize as Timbo, lips tight, eyes blazing, stalked past him on the way to the pavilion. As if still hypnotized by that piece of folly Blake barely moved his bat at all when facing the second ball of the next over and was unarguably lbw. Trimdon were two wickets down with just 5 on the board.

'Oh no!' Lawrie groaned again in complete despair. 'I'll have to go, I'm in next! Just pray that Steve and the skipper put on a record stand for this wicket!'

Nick was hoping that, too. What had also dismayed him was that Luke Penhale had picked up his first wicket from a not particularly impressive delivery. The ball had been straight and fairly fast, but any reasonably alert batsman ought to have been able to play it comfortably.

Lawrie's prayers were not answered. Steven played himself in with his usual assurance but Craig rarely seemed at ease after fending off a couple of bouncers, one of which very nearly provided the wicketkeeper with a spectacular catch as he fell backwards, arms at full stretch. As if in relief at his escape, the Trimdon captain turned a ball off his toes for a rasping boundary, but in the following over his luck ran out and he played on to a full-length delivery from Luke.

Nick gritted his teeth; his rival had now collected two wickets and was looking better with every over he bowled. Worse, of course, Trimdon were now only 25 for 3. Craig's dismissal was greeted with unreserved acclaim by Wheathouse and their supporters while a collective silence appeared to have fallen over the Trimdon camp. Johnny Highton was saying nothing to anyone as he slumped in a colourful deck-chair kindly provided by his opposite number who'd admitted earlier he liked 'a bit of old-fashioned style about the proceedings'.

'If it goes on like this I'll be batting in the next few minutes,' Nick remarked dolefully to Adam who nodded and said, equally despondent, 'And I could be joining you!'

There was still no sign of his mother or of Kamran and Nick was beginning to worry that they'd arrive when he himself was bowling with Trimdon having put up the sort of total that couldn't possibly be defended.

'Come on, you two, get stuck in – give me *something* to bowl at,' he muttered just under his breath.

Lawrie's nerves, however, soon overcame him. Caught in two minds about how to deal with a sharply rising ball he really made no sort of stroke at all and presented the bowler with the easiest of catches. The score had reached only 32 and worse was to follow for Jack Songhurst was out to the first ball he received. Admittedly, it was a superb out-swinger that deceived him and which would have troubled a far better batsman than the Trimdon wicketkeeper. As it was, he swished at it hopefully, got an edge and the ball was eagerly seized by his opposite number: 32 for 5.

Nick had barely started to strap on his pads when Jack's wicket fell. The collapse was becoming a catastrophe and he gulped at the thought of the responsibility now resting on him and Steven Lindley.

'Go out and do your stuff,' Craig told him. 'Don't panic whatever you do. The rest of 'em seem to have a death wish. Keep us alive, Nick!'

Plainly the crisis had affected Craig, too, for that wasn't his usual injunction.

Nick nodded that he understood. Deliberately he took his time in walking out to bat. As he glanced round the ground, he suddenly caught sight of Denis Demarco, lolling against a tree trunk. So his best friend had arrived on time for once! He waved his bat at him and got a raised thumb from Denis in response. Somehow, that familiar gesture added to Nick's sense of well-being. He knew from his own experience how the bowler would be feeling: almost pantingly impatient to get on with the destruction. And, it suddenly occurred to Nick, probably desperate to achieve a hat-trick!

'Well, he's not going to get *me*,' Nick told himself. 'I'll go for him!'

He'd been thinking earlier about how he would deal with his real rival, Luke Penhale, if he had to face him. Attack, it had often been drummed into him by his mother, was the best form of defence. Well, Trimdon were on the defensive and so this could be the moment to put that theory into practice. His aim had to be to drive Luke out of the firing line. First, though, he had to survive the hat-trick ball. Almost inevitably, the bowler, bedazzled by the sudden prospect of glory, lost his control. Presented with the easiest of half-volleys, Nick stepped out and drove the ball imperiously through the covers for a doubly satisfying boundary. He'd avoided disaster and was convincingly off the mark. Steve patted his bat in approval and that gesture seemed to endorse Nick's resolution to carry the fight to the enemy.

After Steven had snicked a single in the next over, Nick faced Luke. Luke, too, recognized the opportunity to up-stage his rival as well as add to his tally of wickets. Moreover, he'd spotted Kamran Aslam's arrival and he wanted to demonstrate to the Test player that he was the best young fast bowler in the county. Nick, concentrating totally on his batting, was unaware of Kamran's presence. In any case, it wasn't really with the bat that he wanted to impress.

As Luke purposefully strode back to his bowling mark, Nick took a couple of sideways steps down the wicket. He was now standing well out of his ground but that was all part of his strategy. Then, as Luke raced in, Nick glanced back to see whether the wicketkeeper, previously standing well back, had moved forward. He hadn't. So all was well. The ball could have been one of Luke's best, a swinging yorker, but to Nick it seemed no more than a full toss. He swung – and hit – and the ball positively hurtled back down the pitch past the astonished bowler. The nearest fielder, too, was so startled that he had no real chance of cutting off a boundary.

Nick glowed. He didn't need the applause from the Trimdon team and supporters to tell him what a good stroke it was and how much of a psychological advantage it had already given him over Luke Penhale. Once again, Steven signalled congratulations. If he had any doubt about Nick's tactic of moving down the pitch he kept it to himself. It wasn't his policy to undermine his partner's confidence in any way.

Luke reacted in the way Nick expected and might well have reacted himself. He whipped down a bouncer, but Nick, still down the pitch, whirling, hit it on the rise and struck the first six of the match. It was utterly exhilarating. This time the applause from the supporters was almost frenzied. Even Mr Highton, sitting upright in his chair, joined in. Then it became all the better for the hero of the moment when he caught a glimpse of Kamran who'd stationed himself beside the sight-screen. He was clapping as vigorously as anyone.

Nick was remembering a match about a year ago when a batsman adopted the same strategy when facing him. At first he'd succeeded in unsettling Nick's rhythm and forcing him to bowl differently. The batsman's stance meant that the angle of attack had to be changed because of where the slips and keeper were standing in relation to him. It hadn't occurred to Nick to demand support from his skipper in moving the keeper up to the stumps, but eventually he'd outwitted the batsman by bowling him a slower ball he'd missed completely. Now Nick had his fingers crossed Luke wouldn't try the same expedient.

The next ball was pitched shorter, kept low and Nick couldn't adjust his stroke before it rapped his pads. Luke, spinning like a dervish, roared his appeal for a dismissal but Nick knew he'd have to be very unlucky to be given out lbw because he was so far down the wicket. All the same, he was relieved when the umpire murmured 'Not out'.

In only five overs the Trimdon score advanced to 74 and Nick got 30 of them, including the six and four fours. He was beginning to believe that not only would he get the highest score of his career but he'd turn it into a maiden half-century. It proved to be fatal thinking. Luke, having suffered the severest punishment from Nick's bat, was replaced by an off-spinner. In his euphoria, Nick forgot that he no longer needed to be standing out of his crease. So, when he missed a sharp turner, the wicketkeeper, standing close up again, had no difficulty in flicking off the bails in a very competent bit of stumping.

Nick grimaced and cursed silently. He knew he shouldn't have begun to think about his own score, but the possibility of collecting his first 50 couldn't be shut out. Steven, who'd been accumulating runs in his usual careful fashion, called: 'Bad luck. But well done. We're back in the match, you know.' Nick's one personal consolation was that it wasn't Luke Penhale who'd taken his wicket.

'Oh, Nick, you've let me down!' his mother greeted him as he approached the pavilion. 'The moment I arrive, you get yourself out! And everyone here's saying what a great knock it was. So, well done. If only . . .'

'Thanks,' he said, grateful that she didn't offer to kiss him in front of team-mates applauding him in. At least his innings had distracted spectators from taking too much notice of her appearance, he reflected. He found the admiring looks and wolf-whistles she invariably attracted highly embarrassing, though his mother seemed to take them all in her stride.

Kamran raised a thumb and Nick cheerfully acknowledged it. He wondered whether he should now stroll across to chat to his hero but he didn't want anyone, particularly Mr Highton, to suppose that he was interested only in mixing with the famous (or, indeed, put the idea into someone's mind that he himself had invited Kamran Aslam to the match). The Test player was already surrounded by a variety of people, some of whom wanted his autograph or to be photographed with him.

The Wheathouse College captain decided that Nick's departure was the moment to bring Luke back into the attack in place of his fellow opening bowler and it proved to be a shrewd decision. In a matter of minutes the Trimdon innings had folded for a total of 90.

Adam Lexton laid about him for a couple of overs but no one else managed any runs at all, and Steven was unlucky because he couldn't even get the strike. He remained 30 not out, which meant that Nick was joint top scorer. Nick's other source of satisfaction was that Luke managed to pick up only one more wicket, the off-spinner garnering the rest with his well-flighted and accurate deliveries.

'Poor showing; should have done better than that,' murmured Johnny Highton, rising from his chair at last. 'But at least you did the right thing, young Nick. Showed real enterprise, taking on their fast fella like that. Well done!'

Nick blinked. He couldn't help it. Old Highbrow was praising him again! 'Thanks, sir,' he managed to respond.

Craig took up the same theme, pleased that his own failure was not being mentioned. 'Maybe it's your day, Nick. So go on with the good work. You destroyed their attack, so now you can destroy their batters. Destroyer Freeland, firing on all cylinders – or something like that.'

Sallie Freeland, who was within earshot and apparently chatting with an acquaintance, glanced across at him and smiled. 'Well done,' she mouthed, and Nick could read her lips. 'Keep it up!'

He felt immensely heartened by the chorus of praise. Then, as he turned away to go into the pavilion before Trimdon took the field, he saw Kamran detach himself from his circle of admirers, signal with a wave and come towards him.

'Great! I really enjoyed your batting,' the Test star

exclaimed, draping an arm round Nick's shoulders. 'Glad I wasn't the bowler – you'd have smashed me all over the place the way you were going. Oh yes, and I'll get you an ice-cream to celebrate next time. Pity no one's selling any here today.'

'Thanks, Kamran,' Nick said, scarcely able to believe what he was hearing. Yet he could tell his hero meant what he said; he certainly wasn't patronizing him.

'Now you must do it with the ball to win this match,' Kamran went on. 'I think you will. I think you are like me, Nick, the big occasion brings out the best in you. It *inspires* you. And remember, wrist behind the ball.'

Those words were still revolving in Nick's mind as he marked out his run and the Wheathouse College openers strolled to the wicket. Everyone seemed to have wished him luck and his skipper had suggested it might well be his day. Well, he was determined to make sure it was. His batting had been good; but his bowling was going to be even better. If Trimdon were to win this match and stay in the Cup then they *must* take early wickets.

He took his time over his practice run and again when he bowled a trial ball to Adam who duly lobbed it back. Already the senior umpire had given him an inquiring look and called 'Play!'

Nick came in at very nearly his fastest. The moment the ball left his fingers he *knew* it was right – that it would pitch on a length, fizz inwards and tuck the batsman up. In fact, the batsman was nowhere near good enough to deal with it for he'd never received a first ball of the match as good as this one. Making no adjustment whatsoever, he lifted his arms to let the ball go by and was horrified to see his middle stump knocked flat.

There was a moment of stunned disbelief before the Trimdon team started to leap about and rush to congratulate the bowler. Shaking his head, the batsman trudged back to the pavilion. His replacement was inclined to treat the dismissal as a fluke. No bowler could repeat that sort of delivery with his very next ball.

But the second delivery proved to be faster even than the first. This time there was hardly any movement off the seam at all. The batsman, bat held high as if to hit anything he received out of the ground, was far too late in jabbing it down to protect his legs. And the umpire's finger was rising for lbw practically before Nick could complete his appeal.

'Two in two – brilliant!' yelled Lawrie, racing over from deep mid-wicket to fling his arms round Nick. 'We're back in the match. Go on, Destroyer, make it a hat-trick!'

Nick didn't really want to say anything to anyone. He knew that his mum and Kamran and probably even old Highbrow would be applauding and urging him on. But he didn't want to be distracted. All his concentration had to be devoted to sending down another ball as good as the first two deliveries. He knew that the newcomer was called Inman, Wheathouse's star player. Nick had to remove him as quickly as possible. But the pun came into his mind and he couldn't help grinning: Not Inman, *Out*man!

Craig had ordered his fielders to close in. If ever there were a moment to set an attacking field, this was it.

Inman, tall, elegant, apparently unruffled by what had gone before and unworried about facing a hat-trick ball, told himself that by the law of averages the next ball couldn't be as good. He would attack it because that was his nature; he must demonstrate that he was the batsman to master any bowler. So he drove, or attempted to drive, another good-length ball. But he was a fraction too soon, got an edge and, with rare nonchalance, Jack Songhurst took the catch to complete Nick Freeland's hat-trick.

Inman closed his eyes, sagged mentally and physically and turned away.

This time the celebrations were prolonged until the umpire, becoming exasperated, said, 'This is not a football match, you know. The bowler's done well but he knows that by now. Let's get on with the cricket.'

Nick was grateful for that intervention and the chance to resume his over without further delay. He didn't think he could keep this up; the impossible dream was really happening, happening to him, happening in front of his coach and his hero and his team-mates. He'd never achieved a hat-trick before – and it was on a day he'd avoided being a hat-trick victim himself and gone on to make his highest score with the bat.

The new batsmen were taking longer and longer to reach the wicket. The No. 5 one looked nervous and bemused, as he was entitled to in the circumstances. Nick, staring at him and *willing* him to get out, sensed it was the moment to try his slower ball. Everyone, including the batsman, would be expecting the fastest.

It worked.

Like Inman before him, the new Wheathouse batsman decided to hit out. He, too, swished too soon, sending the ball steepling above the middle of the wicket. Nick never took his eyes off it. 'Mine!' he yelled as he trotted forward and caught the falling ball.

Nick now had time to experience the strangest of sensations, elation mixed with wonderment, before Craig crashed into him in his own exultation.

'Four wickets in four balls! Fantastic! Four for none! They'll never recover from this, Nick. You've won us the match in the first over!'

He had. Wheathouse didn't recover. They were all out for 42. Nick took only two more of the six wickets that fell as demoralized Wheathouse crumbled to defeat.

That didn't matter. With four wickets in the first four balls of the innings, Nick Freeland had gained a place in the record books for the first time. And everybody watching his extraordinary achievement sensed it wouldn't be the last time, either.